Elise's New Song

Crawdad Beach Series (Book 10)

Lisa Buffaloe

Elise's New Song

John 15:11 Publications

This novel is a work of fiction. Names, characters, places, towns, singers, lawyers, police officers, medical and security personnel, enormous cats, crawdads, and all people and incidents are the product of the author's overactive imagination and used fictitiously.

Any resemblance to actual events, persons living or dead, or any other person, including any place or thing, is entirely coincidental and beyond the author's intent.

No crawdads or enormous cats were injured in the making of this novel.

Visit the author's website at https://lisabuffaloe.com.

Cover Design: JoAnn Durgin

ISBN: (eBook) 978-1-957715-43-8
ISBN: (Paperback) 978-1-957715-44-5
ISBN: (Hardcover) 978-1-957715-45-2

WELCOME
to
Crawdad Beach
South Carolina

Elise's New Song

Elise Thomas is no longer the singer with crazy makeup, outfits, and wild hair designs. Those days are long gone. God has given her a new life, and she's ready to fade quietly into the background.

Thankfully, Crawdad Beach is over two thousand miles from her past. But will the distance be enough?

Richard Worthington III works hard for his success. Although Crawdad Beach is a small town, the chance to have his name on the sign of his own law firm is an opportunity Richard can't refuse.

And, if his plans for success continue, someday, everyone will know his name.

Book 10 of the Crawdad Beach Series

Each book in the Crawdad Beach series may be read as a standalone.

"He lifted me out of the pit of despair,
out of the mud and the mire. He set my feet on
solid ground and steadied me as I walked along.
He has given me a new song to sing, a hymn of
praise to our God. Many will see what he has done
and be amazed. They will put their trust in the
Lord. Oh, the joys of those who trust the Lord."
(Psalm 40:2-4a, NLT)

Table of Contents

Chapter 1

In the early morning light, Elise Thomas checked out the window of her hotel room overlooking the Main Street of Crawdad Beach. Her mom was right; the town was charming with a fun sense of humor.

Neatly maintained, two-story buildings lined the brick-paved road. Besides a law office, post office, and two buildings with loft apartments, the town sported Knick Knacks Antique store, Curl and Dye Beauty Salon, Tiddlywinks Restaurant, and Rolling in the Dough Bakery. She grinned at the Doohickeys Hardware Store sign that said they proudly offered a wide range of hardware, building supplies, and whatever whatchamacallit needed.

Ten years ago, Elise couldn't wait to leave a small town. Now, she craved a simpler, quieter life.

Crawdad Beach was over two thousand miles from Los Angeles, but would the distance be enough? With all her mistakes and the issues that came with her previous life, could she really start over?

Dressed in jeans and a comfy top, Elise pulled her long blonde hair into a ponytail, took her purse, and locked her hotel room behind her.

If all went well, no one would know who she used to be. She was just Elise Thomas, and that was fine with her.

Richard Worthington hung his last diploma on the wall. The old oak floors creaked as he stepped back to ensure the document was straight. At twenty-eight, he'd secured his goal of owning a law firm. He looked around his office, smelling of wood, leather, and antique law books.

A soft knock on the side of the open door frame announced Carlton McGee's entrance. "Are you getting settled?" Carlton, a good friend of Richard's dad, was retiring and had invited Richard to take over his practice.

The big man came toward him. "I'm grateful Cora has agreed to stay. She's part secretary, paralegal, and an all-around office whiz. Cora will be a great help to you, as she has been to me throughout the years." Carlton ran his hand through his white hair, then pointed toward the bookshelves. "Remove anything you don't want to keep."

Richard glanced at the bounty of law books. "I'm honored to keep everything you've collected over the years."

"Good. I was hoping you would say that. My wife will be ecstatic that I won't bring them home. She's ready to downsize the house and travel the country."

Richard gave the man a kind smile. "I can't tell how much I appreciate your faith in me to take over your business."

"I don't doubt you will be a wonderful lawyer for my Crawdadian friends."

"It will be a new experience working in a town with a cartoon crawdad as a mascot."

Carlton's eyes twinkled with a hint of mischievousness as he laid a hand on Richard's shoulder. "All that happens in our little town might surprise you. I could write volumes on the subject. Crawdad Beach isn't next to the ocean, but we have lots going on behind the scenes. Since God brought you here, He has something amazing planned for you."

"I guess we'll see about that." Richard removed his glasses and rubbed the bridge of his nose. He'd stopped talking to God a few years ago. Besides, God didn't bring him here. It was Richard's family connections and his hard work.

Crawdad Beach was only a stepping stone. And if all his plans worked out, someday, everyone would know the name of Richard Worthington, the third.

Chapter 2

After spending the day with the Realtor, Elise sat at her hotel room desk and spread out the information on the homes she'd viewed.

She dropped the flyer for the house with fifty acres into the trash can. The home needed significant updating, and that much property might be challenging to maintain. Another house on ten acres was a possibility. But could she feel safe by herself in the country? Elise tossed the flyer.

Properties in the town's city limits were older and reasonably decent, but did she want to be that close to other people? Her Realtor, Fushia Gates, didn't live in Crawdad Beach, yet she gushed about how friendly the townspeople were.

After weeks of fervent prayer for guidance on whether to leave California, Elise had felt a divine pull towards the small South Carolina town. The verse she kept close to her heart was Exodus 33:14, in which God told Moses that His presence would go with Moses and give him rest.

Since deciding to move, Elise felt a lightness in her step, a sense of calm, like a heavy weight had lifted off her shoulders.

Tomorrow morning, she'd view a Victorian house that came with extra property close to downtown and supposedly had great potential. Maybe living within the city limits wouldn't be too bad.

Returning to California wasn't an option. She'd sold her house and car in Los Angeles and placed her belongings in storage. Being in the limelight had its perks but came with more problems than most people could imagine. Elise couldn't take the chance of another deranged fan coming after her. She shuddered and shook off that troubling memory.

Tennessee was her home state. As much as Elise loved her family and the beauty of her hometown, living too close to her parents wouldn't work. During her rockstar days, social media had blasted much of her private details to the world. Plus, she was too ashamed of her past behavior.

She'd removed as much of her information from the internet as possible and used a service to forward any mail sent to her stage name. As far as most people knew, she still lived in California.

Prompted by her grumbling stomach, Elise put aside the real estate papers. Mrs. Gates had recommended Tiddlywinks Restaurant's excellent country cooking. That thought made her mouth water.

Stepping onto the Main Street sidewalk, Elise took a few minutes to check her surroundings. A nice-looking middle-aged couple walking hand-in-hand greeted her as they sauntered past. Other people of various ages looked like they were shopping or running errands.

Thankfully, no one seemed interested in her. Not that they should now. Her days in the limelight were over.

Elise glanced at Rolling in the Dough. Tomorrow morning, she'd grab a bite at the bakery. Hopefully, after she returned from house hunting, she could wander around the antique and hardware stores.

Her attention returned to the sidewalk. Coming toward her was a curly brown-haired guy walking the biggest cat she'd ever seen. Seriously? A cat on a leash?

She grabbed her phone and took a quick photo to send to her cat-loving mom.

With a sudden, powerful jerk, the feline strained against the man's grip, sending him stumbling as he fought to regain control.

The small mountain lion-sized cat ran toward her and vaulted straight into her arms. Elise struggled to keep hold of his big, furry body. He nestled against her chest and purred the loudest purr she had ever heard. Unsure how to react, she stared into the cat's massive, furry face.

"I'm sorry!" The guy tried to take the cat, but the animal only snuggled closer to her. He gave her a confused expression. "Do you know Sir Purrcevel?"

Elise chuckled at the weird situation and the name. "I don't believe I've had the pleasure before now of meeting Sir Purrcevel."

"That's strange. He's not usually this forward or friendly."

"Don't worry." Elise rubbed the cat's soft fur with her free hand. "I'm an animal lover." Was he part Persian and part mountain lion?

As though Sir Purrcevel understood her comment, he stared lovingly at her.

"I can't believe this." A dark brown-haired woman about Elise's age, wearing medical scrubs, hurried toward them. "Sir Purrcevel, you big flirt." Her big brown eyes turned to Elise. "I'm Paige Young, and I guess you've met my husband, Quinn, and our very forward cat."

Elise took a moment to respond. In Los Angeles, she would have wondered why the couple were being friendly and what they wanted from her. But now, she needed to act like she used to as a kid back in her hometown. "It's nice to meet you. I'm Elise Thomas."

"Are you visiting or staying in Crawdad Beach?" Paige asked.

"I guess you could say both. I'm visiting for now, but also looking for a place to live."

The big cat purred louder.

"That's wonderful. You will love it here. A house down the street from us is for sale." Paige grinned. "If you find something you like that needs work, Katherine Mitchell is our local renovator extraordinaire. She renovated our house and most of the buildings downtown."

"Speaking of Katherine," Quinn waved at an older white-haired gentleman with a little black and white dog crossing the street and walking toward them. "There's her dad, Henry Doss."

Sir Purrcevel jumped out of Elise's arms and ran straight toward the little dog.

Elise grimaced at what might happen when the two animals met. Instead, the dog wagged like crazy, and Sir Purrcevel rubbed against his fur. "Since when did dogs and cats become friends?"

"These two are big-time buddies," Quinn said. "They play hide and seek, chase one another around the house, and play fetch."

Elise couldn't believe the affection between the animals.

"Hello." The white-haired man's blue eyes radiated kindness as he gazed at Elise. "You're new here. I'm Henry Doss." He pointed toward his dog. "This is Filbert."

"Hi, Mr. Doss and Filbert." She shook the man's outstretched hand and gave Filbert a pat on his furry head. "I'm Elise Thomas."

"She's going to be moving to town," Paige said. "We were telling Elise about your daughter, Katherine."

"That's great news. Welcome to Crawdad Beach."

Paige shifted her gaze back to Elise. "Would you like to join us for dinner? After we walk Sir Purrcevel home, we're going to eat at Tiddlywinks."

"I'll take Sir Purrcy home with me," Henry said. "The animals can play until you get back from dinner."

"Thank you, Henry. That's sweet of you."

"My pleasure."

The cat and dog strolled side by side as Henry led them away.

Elise grinned. If Crawdad Beach was half this entertaining, she definitely had found her new home.

Richard shook his head at the little cartoon crawdad wearing a chef's hat at the top of Tiddlywinks' restaurant menu. It seemed every store in town, including the library and the medical clinic, used a crawdad in murals or as a logo.

He would *not* use a crawdad for his law office. How could anyone take him seriously if he used a cartoon mascot?

Unfortunately, the more he tried not to think about that possibility, the more images came to mind. He could picture a crawdad wearing a long black robe sitting at a judge's bench, or one holding the scales of justice, or a crawdad wearing a business suit as though arguing a case in front of a judge.

Richard groaned at his thoughts. He wasn't a kid anymore. He was a professional, and he needed to act like one.

"Could you not find something you liked?" A troubled expression on her face, a cute brunette waitress stared at him.

Richard offered a friendly smile. "No, it's not that. Everything looks great. I was just thinking about something else."

"Oh, I'm so glad. I promise you'll like anything on the menu. George and Faith Hollis are the owners, and they make sure their food is delicious."

"Okay. Thanks." Richard placed his order and then discreetly studied the restaurant patrons. Most of the customers were families or couples. He was the only one dining alone.

His life should have been different. He owned his law firm but wasn't living in a big city and married to the woman of his dreams. God had robbed him of all that.

He forced himself to relax and willed away the unwelcome emotions. His mother kept telling him to count his blessings. Richard internally scoffed. He'd tried that, but God had deserted him when he needed Him the most.

His gaze moved to the door where a couple holding hands and a tall, slender blonde woman made their way to an empty table near him. As the couple and the blonde sat, Richard tried not to stare. Besides being gorgeous, the woman looked vaguely familiar.

Her blue-gray eyes flitted momentarily toward him, then back toward her friends.

He forced his attention back to his table. If his younger brother, John, had been here, he'd have said, "Yowza, what a woman!" John had always been the more outgoing, happy-go-lucky guy who never hesitated to talk to any woman he met. His gregarious personality had netted him a job in a major law firm, with a sweet wife and two kids.

Why was his brother given what he wanted?

Richard rubbed the back of his neck. Everything that happened to him was more proof that God was not fair.

The server brought his food and set it in front of him. Richard thanked her and picked up his fork.

At least now he could eat and stop thinking about cartoon crawdads, beautiful women, his brother, and God.

Chapter 3

Elise waited while her Realtor unlocked the door of the historic home in the oldest section of Crawdad Beach.

The middle-aged woman's multiple bracelets jangled as she turned the key. She grinned over her shoulder at Elise. "Built in 1905, the house features Victorian architectural details with a wraparound porch and is fully enclosed by an ornamental iron fence for privacy."

As they stepped inside, Mrs. Gates made a sweeping gesture with her hand. "Just look at the beautifully detailed woodwork, elegant winding staircase, lovely hardwood floors, soaring ceilings, grand fireplaces, and traditional decorative diamond-shaped large windows. With over 3,000 square feet, it's a perfect blank canvas for your dream home."

Elise grinned at the woman's enthusiasm. During the house tour, she made mental notes of what would be required to get it to a comfortable, livable level. It did have potential, but the floors needed refinishing, and the walls had tattered wallpaper or peeling paint. Bathroom fixtures would need updating, and the roof needed to be replaced. The electrical, heating, and air systems would require a complete overhaul.

Elise loved the house, but was she up for an extensive

project like this? She had the time and funds, knew most of the construction basics, and could do many projects herself. While her grandad was alive, after school and during the summer, she'd been one of his employees, helping him build and renovate houses.

"I realize this home needs some work," Mrs. Gates said. "It's been empty for five years, but we have a wonderful builder and renovator in town, Katherine Mitchell."

"I've heard about Katherine."

"Oh, honey, she's the best. Whatever you need done, Katherine can do it, or she will hire someone for you. The Crawdadians take good care of one another." Mrs. Gates turned to face Elise and leaned close. "May I ask you a personal question?"

Her pulse notching upward, Elise tried not to react. "Of course."

"You look a little like that singer with the funny stage name who wore all that wild makeup."

Elise kept a neutral expression. "I've heard we have similarities."

"Yes." Mrs. Gates leaned closer. "You resemble her a little. Maybe it's your height and pretty eye color. But you're much more attractive. She always wore lots of makeup, had a spiky haircut, and dressed weirdly."

Elise wrinkled her nose. "Her style was a little much, wasn't it?"

"Yes, but she did have a pretty voice."

Elise turned away and pretended to study the woodwork. She did not miss the makeup, clothes, and the life she'd led, but she'd always miss her singing voice.

Mrs. Gates motioned for her to follow her out the back door. "I've saved the best for last."

A wave of tranquility washed over Elise as she stepped onto the back porch and viewed the most beautiful, well-maintained, pristine garden she'd ever seen.

The layout reminded her of a smaller version of the ones she'd visited when she toured Europe. Sunlight filtered from massive oak trees beside the garden area. A winding path led toward a white octagon-shaped gazebo at the garden's center.

The gazebo's shingled roof raised to a cupola, and inside the structure sat two white wicker chairs, inviting visitors to sit and enjoy the beauty.

Neatly trimmed small hedges ran alongside the pathway. Symmetrical flower beds filled with blooming flowers lay behind. Large hedges over six feet tall rimmed the perimeter, creating a magical private space.

"How is this possible?" Elise turned to Mrs. Gates. "I thought the house had been empty for years."

"It has, but the gardener never left." She pointed to an iron gate at the back of the property. "He lives in the small cottage in the back."

Wondering if that was creepy, Elise gulped. "Someone still lives here?"

"Oh yes, from the notes on the listing, he's been here

quite some time."

"Does someone pay his salary?"

Mrs. Gates tapped a manicured finger against her chin. "I'm not sure. The woman who lived here died five years ago. It's funny; we've had people look at the house and make offers, but the company that owns the property never would approve of the people who wanted to make a purchase."

Elise went to the back iron gate and pushed. It opened with a tiny squeak. Flowers lined a walk leading to what looked like an old English cottage. Peace seemed to surround the area. The only thing grounding Elise in the present was a newer model car parked in the gravel driveway.

"The cottage does come with the property." Mrs. Gates stood next to her. "It's lovely, don't you think?"

"It is beautiful."

A dignified-looking gentleman with salt-and-pepper hair and a handlebar mustache stepped out the door. "Ladies, how are you today?"

Elise smiled at the man's proper English accent. "Hello. We're just viewing the house. I'm considering buying the property."

"I thought you would." His blue eyes had a gentleness to them.

"You did?"

"Yes. During my prayer time, I sensed someone would be at the house today to return her to her former glory. Excuse my manners." A warm smile spread across his face as he gave a slight, elegant bow. "I am Ian Hammond at your service."

Elise had to catch herself from doing a curtsy. "Nice to meet you, Mr. Hammond. I understand you live here. But who pays your salary?"

"Salary is of no consequence. I am self-sufficient. Caring for the garden and property has been one of my delightful callings. And please call me Ian."

"Okay, Ian. But taking care of a garden without pay is unusual."

"Perhaps it is. If you buy the property, I will gladly leave or stay."

"I'm not sure yet if I'll buy the house or if I would want you to vacate your home."

"The cottage belongs to the property. Whatever you decide to do about my services will not be a problem." His blue-eyed gaze met hers. "The choice is yours."

The Realtor, with a hopeful expression, peered at Elise. "Well, would you like to come by the office and sign papers?"

"I need time to think about all of this. Ian, it was nice to meet you."

"You too, Elise. Godspeed."

Elise turned to go and stopped. She hadn't told the man her name. Gooseflesh raised on her arms as she hurried to the Realtor's car.

As she buckled in, Mrs. Gates turned to face her. "The English surname Hammond means home protection or high protection."

Elise raised her eyebrows. "Really? How would you know that?"

Mrs. Gates drove toward her office. "My husband's ancestors came from England, and since we plan on visiting there, we've been researching English history. According to one surname website, our last name means road or path. We found the name Hammond, listed below my husband's surname." She turned toward Elise. "Maybe Ian is an angel sent to watch over you."

Elise let out a little laugh. "I don't think he's an angel."

"Wouldn't it be amazing, though?" Mrs. Gates's shoulders scrunched up as she grinned. "He could be a personal home-protecting angel who does gardening. Quite fascinating, I think. I can't wait to get home and tell my husband."

Elise shook her head at the woman. Ian Hammond's striking blue eyes and calming nature were nice. But an angel? Surely not.

Still, who was the man, and how did he know her name?

With a final push, Richard maneuvered his couch into the perfect location in his apartment. He stepped back and surveyed his new, albeit temporary, home. The fact that Crawdad Beach had affordable loft apartments with brick walls, hardwood floors, exposed beamed ceilings, an open top-of-the-line kitchen, a stone fireplace, and French doors leading to a balcony overlooking the main street still baffled him. And with his second bedroom, he had plenty of room for a home office.

Richard walked to the French doors and stepped onto his balcony. Besides the hotel, the Main Street businesses were closed at this time of night. He leaned against the railing and looked up at the star-dotted sky. A gentle breeze curled around him.

Despite his preference for a big-city law practice, he had discovered that small-town living was surprisingly positive. He didn't have to fight traffic. He could walk to work. The shops on Main Street carried almost everything he needed, and the grocery store even stocked local organic meat and produce.

A few years ago, he wouldn't have considered living in a place like Crawdad Beach. Not by himself, anyway. But God had taken away his opportunity for a wife and family, and no one could ever replace the woman he loved.

Richard glared at the night sky, shoved away from the railing, and returned inside.

Chapter 4

Wanting a bite to eat before meeting the Realtor, Elise checked the area before hurrying down the sidewalk.

She stopped under the teal and white awning and opened the door to Rolling in the Dough Bakery. Her mouth instantly watered at the delicious smells of baked goods. She went to the glass front display cases and surveyed the goodies.

A young woman with light brown hair and dark brown eyes greeted her. "Welcome to Rolling in the Dough. Our Crawdad Claws are on sale today." She pointed to a pastry shaped like a crustacean. "It's our version of a Bear Claw."

Who could resist a yummy, sweet dough like that? "Sounds good. I'll take a Crawdad Claw and a cup of black coffee, please."

While the woman prepared her order, Elise admired the mural of a cute cartoon crawdad wearing a teal apron, holding a rolling pin and an oven mitt. A refurbished teal bicycle and a display cabinet of antique bakery tools adorned the other walls.

Customers sat around the bistro tables, talking or eating pastries. No one seemed in a hurry, and other than a few kind smiles in Elise's direction, no one took notice that, at one time, she'd been famous. At least she had for a little while.

The lack of attention would have been terrible when she started in the music industry, but now Elise found it refreshing.

No more trying to please fans, her agent, recording professionals, or the many people who tried to attach themselves to her earlier stardom. And she'd never, ever miss those who had stalked and hounded her, trying to get close.

After filling up on coffee and sweets, Elise took her time walking through the Victorian home. The ornamental six-foot iron fence surrounding the property would give her added security and privacy, and she'd made notes on the fun possibilities of refurbishing a place like this.

The house had plenty of room for her family to visit. She could have her dream kitchen, home office, and studio.

Her voice could no longer soar into the atmosphere, but she had found a quiet niche to use her voice behind the scenes for television and radio and to make audiobook recordings. Thankfully, her career as a Christian songwriter was also doing well, and the charity she'd started was growing and helping more people.

God had taken away something she loved and thought she couldn't live without. Instead, He'd given her new, less stressful, and more fulfilling opportunities.

"What do you think?" Mrs. Gates gave her a hopeful look. "Is this your next home?"

Elise looked up from her notes. "If Katherine can help me

with what needs to be done, the house will be perfect. But I still don't know what to think about Ian Hammond living on the property. He seems very nice, but what's his story?"

"Oh, that's right," Mrs. Gates said. "I meant to tell you I called Henry Doss last night and asked him for the scoop on Ian. Henry has lived here most of his life and knows everyone. Henry said that Ian is an English professor who works at the university by the beach. So, Ian isn't here all the time. He's in and out but loves caring for the garden because he knew the previous owner. Evidently, they were quite close."

"Sounds like an interesting story."

"Oh, yes. I can imagine." Mrs. Gates nodded. "Ian is very private, so I'm not sure we will ever learn much information. But Henry said that Ian was a very nice, honest man, and having him on your property would be a blessing."

"That is good news. Do you think Katherine would talk to me before I make my decision?"

"I'm sure she would." Mrs. Gates took out her phone and typed in a message. "I just texted her asking if she has a moment to stop by." Her phone signaled a quick reply. "You're in luck. She's in town and can be here in a few minutes."

"That's great." Elise had prayed last night that God would lead her to His choice of where she would live. If they renovated the Victorian, it would be amazing. And who could pass up a gorgeous garden with an on-the-property gardener?

A few minutes later, there was a knock before the front

door opened. “Anybody home?”

“Come on in.”

An attractive middle-aged woman with dark hair and beautiful brown eyes entered the house.

“Katherine,” Mrs. Gates hurried toward her. “So good to see you. I want you to meet my client, Elise Thomas. She’d like to talk to you about renovating the house.”

“Elise, I’d be honored to assist you. I’ve always loved this place and hoped someone would want it restored. What do you have in mind?”

Elise gave her the notes she’d taken with her ideas.

Katherine took her time looking them over. “This will be a big job, but a fun one. I’m between renovation projects right now, so if you buy the house, I’ll be ready to go when you need me.”

“Really? That would be wonderful.” Elise turned to Mrs. Gates. “Let’s go write up the paperwork and get started.”

Richard took his time reviewing the case files and documents left in his care. Most of the business in the practice had been estate planning, family law, real estate, business transactions, probating wills, and other basic law needs, with very few criminal cases or divorces.

Carlton’s practice had provided the man a decent living, but it paled compared to what Richard could get in a larger city. Thankfully, he'd been prepared to adjust to his living situation. Since he was sixteen, he'd worked and saved every penny he could. In school, he made sure his grades were top-notch to get scholarships for his education. He remained debt-free, owned his car outright, and his new affordable apartment provided a comfortable living space.

He'd seen how easy it was to get obsessed with money. At the last law firm where he'd worked, the lawyers drove luxurious cars and lived in extravagant homes, flaunting their wealth, while their trophy wives spent money on jewelry, spa days, and plastic surgery.

Richard grimaced at the thought. He wanted to make a name for himself, but not like that. If he ever met another woman to consider as a wife, she'd have to be level-headed and not someone who would waste his hard-earned money.

But could he, and would he, take the chance of ever loving someone again?

Chapter 5

Elise hadn't been this excited in years and barely slept during the night. The seller accepted her cash offer without hesitation, especially since Elise didn't ask for any repairs.

She purchased the house as-is, which suited her perfectly since she was ready to take on a fun project. Her parents were thrilled that she would live within driving distance.

Elise looked forward to a fresh start in Crawdad Beach. Go figure. She was stoked to ditch fame and settle into obscurity. Walking away from her upbringing and faith to pursue worldly success had caused more heartache and pain than she could measure.

Thankfully, God had forgiven her, and today was a new day. Grinning, she checked her look in the hotel mirror. Her hair pulled up in a stylish bun, Elise had chosen a classy V-neck belted short-sleeve dress for the house closing. The neckline was low, but not too low. She never again wanted to use her looks or body in ways that would leave more regrets. She already had enough of those.

With the paperwork signing set for nine o'clock at the law firm, she had plenty of time to get breakfast. As much as Elise enjoyed the food she'd eaten at the bakery, a hardy plate of bacon, eggs, toast, and coffee sounded wonderful.

As soon as the closing ended, she planned to get into casual clothes and work on her new home. After the offer's acceptance, she had called Katherine, and they planned an afternoon get-together to discuss the house project.

Elise stepped out onto the Main Street sidewalk and took a deep breath of the clean summer air. She'd never miss the congestion and smog of the Los Angeles area.

Two young moms pushing strollers greeted Elise as they sauntered past. A faint, sweet scent of baby powder lingered in the air.

"Well, don't you look nice," Henry Doss's smile crinkled the corners of his eyes as he and another man approached.

"Thank you. I'm closing on a house here in town."

"That's wonderful news," Henry said. "Which one did you buy?"

"The Victorian on Shady Lane."

"That's a magnificent house," the other white-haired man said. "Welcome to Crawdad Beach."

"Forgive me." Henry motioned with his hand. "This is my good friend Chester Taylor. Chester, this is Elise Thomas."

"Very nice to meet you." Chester's eyes held warmth and a fun mischievousness that reminded her of her late grandfather.

"If you have time for breakfast, would you like to join us at Tiddlywinks?" Henry asked.

"I would love that. Thank you."

While they ate, the two men told Elise funny, sweet, and incredible stories about Crawdad Beach and the residents.

Who would have ever thought that a little town like this would have found treasure and had people in interesting and unusual professions, including a man known as the Eliminator? Fortunately, they explained he eliminated problems, not people.

"I have had the best time." Elise placed her napkin on the table and stood. "But I'd better get to the law office."

"We're glad God brought you here, Elise," Henry rose to his feet.

"Thank you." Elise's eyes misted at his kindness. "I'm grateful, too."

Chester handed her a business card with his name and phone number. "Let us know if you ever need anything. My wife, Maybelline, is a wonderful cook. We'd love to have you over sometime for a meal."

Henry also gave her his number. "Never hesitate to call. And next time you see Ian, tell him hello for me."

Elise promised she would, thanked the men, and hurried to her closing.

Although this wasn't her first home purchase, this one seemed different. This time, she wasn't buying something to impress others. Hopefully, her new home base would be where she could accomplish things that were actually worthwhile.

Richard blew out a breath as he closed his accounting software. Good thing he saved his money because the outflow for the business was greater than the inflow.

"They're here and waiting in the conference room, Richard." Cora, his assistant, peeked into his open office door.

"Thanks. I'll be right there." He put on his jacket, adjusted his tie, ran a hand through his hair, and walked down the hall. A house closing wasn't exciting, but at least it would put money into the firm's account.

He stepped into the conference room and stopped. A middle-aged woman and the attractive blonde he'd seen at the restaurant sat at the table. The blonde turned toward him, and her blue-gray eyes sparked in recognition.

Richard introduced himself to the ladies.

The middle-aged woman's bracelets jangled as she shook his hand. "I'm Fushia Gates. I'm the Realtor." She handed him her card. "And this is my client, Elise Thomas."

Elise gave him a polite nod. "Nice to meet you."

Even more stunning up close, it took Richard a few seconds longer than it should have to reply. "Nice to meet you. Is everyone here, or are we waiting for someone else?" He refrained from asking if a husband or significant other was involved in the purchase. However, he noted Elise did not wear a wedding band.

"We're ready." Cora laid out the documents. "The seller remotely completed their portion of the paperwork."

Richard maintained his best professional demeanor. Elise seemed comfortable with the transaction, not even blinking an eye when she handed the cashier's check for the full purchase amount.

How did someone close to his age have that kind of cash? Elise seemed pleasant, but why was she buying a home in Crawdad Beach?

Was she one of those trophy wives who had divorced some poor sap and taken his hard-earned money?

Richard shook off his thoughts. He didn't need to be curious about Elise or any other woman. His goals were success, not relationships.

Chapter 6

Was he a jerk?

Richard sat in his office chair, removed his glasses, and placed his head in his hands. At the closing, he thought he had kept a professional demeanor, but from the curious and sometimes narrow-eyed looks Cora kept giving him, he must not have been as polite as he should have been.

He'd made assumptions about Elise without knowing anything about her. When did he become rude and self-centered? He used to have friends and used to date, but he'd pushed everyone away, including God. Where had it gotten him?

Alone.

Miserable.

Shoving out of his chair, Richard put back on his glasses and shut off his computer. He needed to go for a long run and clear his head.

Since there wasn't anything else on the firm's calendar, he thanked Cora for her work and told her he'd pay her for the rest of the day if she wanted to lock up and leave.

He left her sitting in her chair with a stunned expression. Carlton McGee probably wasn't one to leave his office before closing time.

Richard loosened his tie as he walked out the door. He'd already made a mess of things.

He arrived at his apartment, tossed his jacket on the couch, and went to his bedroom. He didn't like who he had become.

Not one bit.

After changing into shorts and a T-shirt, he put on his running shoes. Even if he became the most influential lawyer in the world, it wouldn't change the past.

He locked up his apartment, sprinted down the stairs, out into the afternoon sunshine, and jogged through downtown to the trail that ran by the small river.

The trees above him provided shade, their leaves rustling softly as his shoes crunched on the path. Although he appreciated the opportunity to own a law firm, reality wasn't anything like he'd imagined.

At least while living in Crawdad Beach, he wouldn't have to drive by the accident site. Bile rose in Richard's throat, and he swallowed hard.

The drunk driver, who ran the red light and hit Richard's car on Annie's side, wasn't even hurt. The police and even Annie's family said it wasn't Richard's fault, and there wasn't anything he could have done. But what if he'd picked his girlfriend up earlier or later or gone a different way to the restaurant?

Annie recovered from her injuries, but after the accident,

everything changed. While in the hospital, she took a shine to the Emergency room physician and started dating him, leaving Richard with the ring he'd planned to give her when he asked her to marry him.

To top off the hurt, Annie married the doctor.

Richard cursed under his breath, increased his pace, and glared at the sky. God should have kept the accident from happening, and Annie would be his.

A tree root snagged his foot. He hit the side of a tree with his face before crashing onto his shoulder.

Groaning, Richard struggled to his feet and adjusted his skewed glasses. He ran a hand across his stinging face and pulled back his fingers, tinged in blood.

Great. Just Great.

He messed up his face, but at least his glasses weren't broken. But who would want a scar-faced lawyer? He slumped back, lay in the grass, and stared at the cloudless sky.

In the movies, this is where he would have his come-to-Jesus moment.

But that wouldn't happen.

God had some explaining to do.

Not only did he lose the woman he loved, but his employer had promoted someone less experienced than him, telling Richard he'd allowed his personal problems to hinder his career.

Richard growled. He'd worked his tail off at that law firm. Man, he wanted to punch something. Pulverize it into nothingness.

The sound of footsteps on the trail brought him to a seated position.

A young woman with a lightning bolt shaved in her short black hair jogged toward him. "You okay?"

"Yeah, I'm fine." Richard stood and brushed himself off.

She continued to jog in place. Her nose wrinkled as she studied him. "Your face looks like it could use some help. The medical clinic is open."

"Thanks. I'm fine."

"Aren't you the new lawyer? I'm Alexis."

"Yes." He attempted a more dignified stance. "Nice to meet you. I'm Richard."

She gave his hand a firm shake. "Welcome to Crawdad Beach. My husband is Tony. He's the big guy who works at Mitchell's grocery store."

Not sure why she was giving him all that information. He gave her a polite nod. "Good to know."

"Well, I hope your day gets better." With a wave, Alexis jogged away.

The townspeople were friendly, but that didn't change what happened. Richard shot another glare at the sky.

The conversation with God wasn't over.

He still wanted answers.

"You think you can fix that?" Elise stood beside Katherine as they surveyed her new home's drooping ceiling.

"I know we can. The roof will be replaced anyway, so that won't be any trouble."

"Great." Elise went down the hall and paused at the top of her stairs. "I'll be here every day trying to get as much done as possible, like removing old wallpaper, sanding woodwork, painting, removing broken bathroom tiles, and other small projects. You sure you don't mind me working alongside you?"

"No, it's your house and your project. You said you used to work with your builder grandad. I've always loved this kind of work, so having another woman along is a bonus."

Elise scrunched her shoulders. "I'm excited."

"Me too. I appreciate you wanting to help."

"Thanks. But do me a favor. If I get in your way, please let me know."

"I promise. The women and men who work on my team are a talented, dependable group. You won't have to worry about being alone in the house with them."

"I appreciate knowing that. I've had trouble before with people." Why did she say that?

Katherine's right eyebrow raised. "If anyone ever makes you feel uncomfortable, let me know. Okay?"

"I will. Thanks."

"I'll be back with the work crew in the morning, and we'll get started."

Elise waited until Katherine left, then went to the dining room to remove the faded, sagging wallpaper.

Her thoughts went to the tall, handsome, dark-haired lawyer at her house closing. Richard Worthington seemed arrogant, yet behind his glasses, his brown eyes carried sadness or disappointment. What happened to him?

Tamping down the desire to help the man, Elise tried to focus on stripping off the old wallpaper. She didn't need to get involved with anyone, especially not someone who was dealing with their own problems. She had enough issues she was still trying to work through.

But one thing she would do was pray for Richard Worthington, the Third.

Chapter 7

Ignoring his aching feet, Richard kept going. He'd already run three times on the river trail, and now he jogged through the neighborhood streets of Crawdad Beach.

His exhausted body wanted to rest, but he wasn't ready to stop. Late evening cast shadows before him as he turned down another road.

Family and friends had pushed him to get over Annie and what happened with his job, telling him that other opportunities would come along.

He now had his own law firm, but it seemed only a hollow victory. He wasn't in a big city law practice with his name on the banner, and Annie wasn't by his side.

He'd show his dad, his old boss, Annie, and the rest of them that Richard Worthington was a man of success.

He passed a house, the scent of freshly cut grass and barbecue mingling with kids' carefree laughter echoing from the backyard. Richard growled. His chance at love had come and gone.

Fisting his hands, he pushed forward. He grew up in church and believed God was good, kind, and loving.

That was before his life fell apart.

Catching his breath by an old Victorian that reminded him of his great-grandparents' massive North Carolina home. The house looked deserted except for a faint light coming from somewhere on the first floor.

Strange.

Was someone living here?

Richard checked the front, but no car was there. A For Sale sign lay on the grass next to the iron gate. Perhaps a Realtor left a light on while showing the house.

Even though he didn't need something this big, exploring the old building would be fun. He stepped to the closed iron gate and pushed.

Surprisingly, it opened without a sound.

Kneeling on the floor, Elise tugged at a stuck, stubborn wallpaper edge next to the baseboard. She should have come better prepared with a steamer or something that would make this easier. All she had to use was an old, dull silverware knife she'd found. It felt good getting rid of the old stuff to make room for the new.

Shame that didn't work that easily in her own life. She'd been the messy one and in need of repair. Why God ever took her back still amazed her. She didn't deserve His forgiveness, not after all her sinful actions. Elise used the dull knife to pry up the wallpaper's edge.

If only she could return to when she was eighteen and make better decisions. Thinking she knew best, Elise had ignored the advice from her parents and friends she should have trusted. Instead, she drove to Los Angeles, toured with bands, and partied with people she should have avoided.

Even worse, as her popularity lessened, she did practically anything to try to stay in the limelight, leaving behind a string of poor decisions and bad relationships. She shook her head at her ignorance and stupidity.

If her voice hadn't failed her, her life would have been an even bigger mess. The change from a star to a nobody had been excruciating, but it had opened her eyes to see how hollow her life had become. Fortunately, when she crawled back to God, He had graciously welcomed her into His grace.

Gripping the corner of the wallpaper, she pulled. It ripped free from the wall, from floor to ceiling. Yes!

She threw the paper into the corner where she'd been stashing the carnage. Tomorrow morning, she'd swing by the hardware store and get supplies, maybe even pick up a big box of pastries for the work crew.

Elise looked out the side window. When did it get dark? Maybe she could finish one more wall before going back to her hotel. From what people told her, Crawdad Beach was a safe town, so she should be fine walking back to her room at night.

Still, Elise wished she'd driven the SUV she purchased when she landed in South Carolina.

The sound of her front door opening stopped her dead in her tracks.

Another sound followed, like the squeak of a tennis shoe.

A cold sweat prickled on her skin. Elise gripped the kitchen knife.

Chapter 8

"Eeeeeeeeeeeeeeeeeeeya!" A crazed woman holding a knife lunged toward him.

Richard held up his hands as he backed away.

The woman stopped. "Richard Worthington?"

He blinked a few times. "Elise Thomas?" She looked different but still attractive in scruffy jeans and an oversized T-shirt. "What are you doing here?"

"This is my house." She jabbed the knife in his direction. "What are *you* doing here?"

Her house? "I thought it was empty."

Elise's eyes narrowed. "You were at my closing and handled all the documents."

He grimaced. "I didn't pay attention to the address." Man, he needed to get his act together.

She scoffed out a breath and again thrust the knife in his direction. "Likely story."

"It's true. Since the door was unlocked, I came inside. The place looked abandoned and reminded me of my great-grandparents' house." Hoping she believed him, Richard lowered his hands. "I'm sorry that I scared you."

When Elise didn't respond, Richard stepped back as she

seemed to process his statements. “I’ll leave you to it.” The sooner he got out, the better.

“Wait.” Elise took a deep breath and slowly released it. “You really just wanted to look around?” A vulnerability lingered in her gaze as she met his.

Richard crossed his heart. “I promise. I did not expect to find you or anyone else here.”

She tapped her foot. A myriad of emotions crossed her face. “You can stay.” She poked the knife toward him again. “But you better behave.”

He attempted to hide his humor at the strange situation, but couldn’t keep it inside. “You’re going to cut me with what looks like a butter knife?”

Elise’s eyes narrowed. She stepped closer. “Laugh all you want, buster, but I could slice you into ribbons.”

Richard gulped and stood still at the seriousness in her eyes. That’s when he heard the faint under-her-breath giggle.

“I was teasing.” Elise backed up. “But I warn you, I have martial arts training.”

“The art of butter knife Jujutsu, huh?”

“You got it.” One of her eyebrows arched. She twirled the knife in her slender fingers. “Not everyone has mastered the technique.”

He held up his hands. “I promise to behave.”

Elise raised her chin. “I’ll give you the benefit of the doubt. Besides that, it looks like your cheek could use some TLC.”

Richard grimaced. He'd forgotten about his messed-up face. "I'm fine. Just the hazard of running while not paying attention."

Elise motioned with her hand. "Follow me. And I'll get you fixed up."

Elise sure hoped Richard was a nice guy. She thought she'd locked the door, but maybe it didn't latch correctly. Tomorrow morning, she'd ask Katherine to install new sturdy locks, and Elise would keep her pepper spray handy.

"Give me a moment." Just in case. She'd let someone know she was alone in her house with a man. Elise texted her mom and told her she was with the lawyer from the closing, Richard Worthington.

Her mom quickly responded with a happy face emoji.

Elise stifled an eye roll. At least her mom wasn't worried.

Richard stood waiting in the foyer, gazing at the ceiling. Scratched face and all, he was a handsome guy with a pleasant sense of humor.

He looked up. "That crown molding shows excellent craftsmanship."

"It is nice," Elise said. "The house needs lots of work, but it does have beautiful potential."

Richard's gaze turned to her. "I am sorry I came into your home without an invitation. Are you sure you're okay with me being here?"

"Not really, but here you are," Elise cringed. Why did she say that? "Sorry. It's just that you surprised me."

Richard cleared his throat. "I'd better go."

"No. Don't go. Let me get your face fixed up." Elise motioned toward the bathroom since someone had kindly left a roll of toilet paper and paper towels.

After he removed his glasses, she tried gently to remove the dried blood from the scratches on his face. He stood still, his gaze locked on the sink in front of them.

Good thing she wasn't the squeamish type since the deepest scratch started oozing blood. She handed Richard a clean paper towel. "You'll need to hold this against your cheek. You might need stitches."

"I hate doctors," he grumbled. "I'll be fine." Richard's eyes softened. "Sorry. Long story. What brought you to Crawdad Beach?"

Elise wadded up the stained paper towels and took them to her trash pile in the dining room. "My mom visited last year and thought it would be a nice place for me to live."

He put on his glasses and gave her a curious expression. "You wanted to live in a small town? Seems an odd place for a single woman to settle."

"Life takes interesting turns." Elise wasn't in the mood to share how she wound up in South Carolina. "How about you?"

"I couldn't pass up the opportunity to own a law firm. The new sign will go up by the end of the week." Richard stood straighter.

"That is impressive. Congratulations."

"Thanks. I hope it's the stepping stone to even bigger things."

"Isn't having your own business arriving at the top?"

He shrugged. "Maybe if the city were larger."

Elise didn't give him her thoughts on that subject. Trying to grasp at something more than what one had could lead to trouble. She learned that the hard way.

Richard headed for the front door. "Sorry again about the intrusion. Are you staying here now?"

"No. The house needs more work. I've got a room at the hotel."

"If you're finished for the night, I can walk with you. My apartment is downtown."

Relieved she wouldn't have to walk in Crawdad Beach alone in the dark, Elise smiled. "I appreciate that offer. I'll take you up on it. Thanks." She locked the door and made sure it stayed secure. Strange that Richard said the door was open.

She gave him a quick glance. During her singing career, she brushed off her discomfort with some people way too often. Some called it a gut feeling; she realized too late that she should have paid attention to God's warnings.

Fortunately, Elise had sensed nothing negative about Richard, but she'd keep alert.

The weight of past mistakes was already heavy enough.

She didn't need to add any more regrets.

Chapter 9

Streetlights lining the roadway cast an inviting glow. A warm breeze rustled the tree leaves as Elise strolled next to Richard.

Why had she been worried about walking back to her hotel? She wasn't a helpless female. Plus, Crawdad Beach had a peaceful vibe during the day and even at night.

Richard glanced her way, his eyes lingering for a moment. "If you don't mind my asking, what are you planning to do while you live here?"

Elise took her time to formulate how she would respond. "I write, do voice work, and a few other things."

"Do you sing?"

Elise kept her voice neutral. "I've done some in the past."

"I can't carry a tune in a wheelbarrow."

"You mean a bucket."

"No. I can't carry a tune in a bucket, wheelbarrow, or dump truck. I was told I have the singing voice of a dying frog."

"Ouch. That wasn't very nice for someone to say."

"Unfortunately, it's true. I used my phone to record myself singing. I sounded like fingernails on a chalkboard."

"I think you have a very nice voice."

"Thank you." Richard gave her a side-eye glance. "I will spare your tender ears the unharmonious cacophony of my singing voice."

Elise liked the version of Richard walking next to her. He seemed more at ease and relaxed. "What do you like to do for fun?"

"Fun?" He paused as though she'd asked a difficult question. It took a few moments for him to respond. "I like to run."

"Does it relax you?"

"Yeah, I guess it does." He resumed walking. "I used to enjoy hiking in the Smoky Mountains."

"I love the mountains." Memories of the majestic mountain ranges she'd seen while on her singing tours ran through Elise's mind. She turned her focus back to the present. "Have you been on any good hikes lately?"

"No. It's been several years."

"Sounds like you need to take a road trip."

"I don't have time. Not now. There's too much to do." Richard's voice took on a different level, more determined. "I'm building my practice in a new place. I've got to advertise, build a good client base, and get involved in the town so people know me."

They turned onto Main Street and continued along the sidewalk.

"Where is the care for the Richard Worthington category?"

He stopped and stared at her like she'd said something ridiculous.

"I'm sorry." Elise held up her hand. "It's none of my business, but I've seen firsthand what happens when someone pushes themselves too hard."

Richard's gaze went to his office across the street. "But, I've got to succeed." His voice was soft, as though he wasn't talking to her.

The way his shoulders slumped, Elise pictured a little boy desperate for affirmation and recognition.

He paused, straightened his posture, and adopted a businesslike expression. "Again, I apologize for entering your house without permission. I did enjoy getting to know you better." Richard stopped outside her hotel.

"Thanks for walking with me. I enjoyed getting to know you better, too. And Richard, no worries about what happened. However, I will ensure my locks work, and I will have more than a butter knife next time I have an unexpected visitor."

He dipped his head. "Have a nice night, Elise."

"You too, Richard."

Elise hurried to her room and peeked out her window. Richard was now standing in front of his office. He ran a hand through his hair, straightened his back, turned, and, head held high, entered his apartment building. She closed the curtains and said a prayer for her new friend.

The next morning, Elise unloaded her SUV with tools for her house project, along with two boxes of pastries and a carafe of coffee from the bakery for the work crew. Today's schedule included Katherine and her employees coming at seven-thirty.

The day passed in a noisy but fun blur. Elise and Katherine had reviewed the job agreement paperwork, and Elise happily paid for the first portion of the work order.

Roofers stripped the old, many-layered shingles off the roof. Katherine and her crew changed out the locks and then worked on the bathrooms and kitchen while Elise continued removing wallpaper.

The construction noises reminded her of the happy times working for her grandad. How different would her life have been if she'd stayed in her hometown and become a builder or renovator? But the past couldn't be changed. Even if it could, she'd have to erase about ten years of her life. At least God was the Master renovator.

"Elise!" Katherine's voice came from upstairs. "We found something you'll want to see."

Hoping it wasn't anything negative, Elise took two steps at a time until she reached where Katherine waited by the small stairs that led to the attic.

"Don't worry, it's nothing bad." Katherine motioned for her to follow. "Look what we found under a loose floorboard."

"Oh, my." Elise carefully lifted a weathered leather-bound book. With a tender touch, she unwound the leather strap that kept the book closed. Yellowed pages crackled as she peeked inside. "It looks like some sort of a journal or diary."

"Is it still legible?" Katherine peered over her shoulder.

"From what I can tell, yes. The writing has faded in some areas but should still be readable under good lighting. Oh my goodness, this is a wonderful prize."

Katherine chuckled. "I know what you'll be doing this evening."

"Thank you so much for finding this."

"My pleasure. We keep our eyes open during any demolition. You never know what might be hiding in older buildings."

Elise stood and hugged the treasure to her chest. "I can't wait to see what someone wrote."

"I'd love to hear what you find out."

"You got it." With her imagination running wild at the possibilities of what she might read, Elise hurried down the stairs. She needed to finish removing wallpaper, but oh, how she wanted to spend the next few days exploring what was written in the journal.

The melodic sound of her doorbell reverberated from the foyer. Goodness, it sounded rather prim and proper. Elise shook herself out of her stupor. The sound meant someone was actually outside waiting.

When she opened the door, Chester and a woman with a

bouffant hairdo stood on her porch. Both of them held what looked like takeout containers.

"Hi, Elise. Remember me, I'm Chester Taylor. And this is my wife, Maybelline."

"Yes, of course, I remember. Maybelline, it's nice to meet you."

"Nice to meet you, too. We wanted to give you an official welcome to Crawdad Beach."

Chester held up what he was carrying. "Maybelline cooked you a meal."

"How nice. Thank you." Elise's mouth watered at the delicious smells wafting from whatever they brought. "Won't you come inside?"

"Thank you, but we don't want to keep you from anything," Maybelline said as they stepped into the foyer beside her.

"What are you holding?" Chester pointed to the journal Elise had in her arms.

"Katherine found this under a floorboard in the attic."

Maybelline moved closer. "Oh, this is a treasure."

Chester peeked over his wife's shoulder. "Maybelline should know. She works at the library."

"You do?" Elise gave the woman a hopeful look. "Do you have one of those big magnifying things with a light attached that I could use?"

"Yes, we do. I'm sure that won't be a problem. I can issue you a library card, check the magnifying light out in your name, and bring it to you this evening."

"That's great. Thank you so much for the food and for offering to bring the light. I'm staying at the hotel downtown. Do you want me to come get it and bring your dishes back?"

"No, that's not a problem. And don't worry about returning the dishes. I buy takeout containers to use when I deliver meals. And I included napkins and plastic silverware."

"Everyone in town knows Maybelline for her amazing cooking," Chester said.

After she thanked the couple and they left, Elise sat on the dining room's hardwood floor and enjoyed Shrimp Creole, rice, and buttery crescent rolls. Sighing, she sat against the wall and surveyed her beautiful new home.

Next, she'd finish removing wallpaper, then drive back to her hotel and explore the once-hidden diary.

Just how much better could her life get?

A familiar ache ran through her chest. With all her past mistakes, would she ever have someone to share her life with?

She didn't deserve God's forgiveness or anything else. God had forgiven her, and that would need to be enough.

Chapter 10

Clutching the diary, Elise fell onto her hotel bed and sobbed into her pillow.

How could Milton leave Rosemary? How could he just walk away after so many moonlit walks in the garden and the many times he pledged his love?

Elise flipped again through the pages of the journal. Their love story could have been a bestseller. Why did Milton leave to make his fortune in New York City? He promised to send for Rosemary as soon as he made enough money. Why didn't he marry her and take her with him?

According to Rosemary's notes, she didn't realize she was carrying his child when he left. In 1936, that would have been a terrible scandal.

Poor, poor Rosemary.

When her family discovered her condition, her father and brother swore they would dispatch Milton from the earth if the man dared to return to Crawdad Beach.

Rosemary made her last entry in February 1936. Her parents were sending her to stay with a distant relative in England to escape the shame of the child she bore. She was only eighteen.

Rosemary's family had no idea that the world was on the brink of World War II.

Elise cried again for the young woman she'd never meet and for the rest of the story that she'd never know.

With a gritty, sandpaper-like sensation burning her eyes, Elise arrived at the Victorian at seven in the morning. She didn't regret staying up most of the night to read the journal, but boy, it was apparent she could no longer run on just a few hours' sleep.

Even the big fat cinnamon roll she'd eaten and the twenty ounces of coffee she'd finished hadn't given her the energy or caffeine kick she needed.

She shuffled into her living room and looked around. There was still so much to do. She wasn't just tired; she was sad. What happened to Rosemary? Did she arrive safely in England?

Were her relatives kind and understanding or cruel? Did Rosemary keep the baby or have to send it off to an orphanage? Did she die at the hand of the Nazis?

Elise shoved a stray hair behind her ear. Maybe if she looked into the house's history, she could find out about Rosemary's family. Yes!

She'd get as much done as possible this morning, then run by the library at lunch and see if Maybelline had any historical information about the previous owners.

The sound of vehicles pulling into her driveway turned Elise's attention. As she watched Katherine and her team walk toward the house, Elise remembered Katherine's dad, Henry Doss, who grew up in the town. Maybe he knew some details about the previous owners.

The crew greeted her and dispersed to work in various parts of the house.

"Katherine, can I talk to you for a moment?" Elise pulled her aside. "Do you know anything about the people who owned this house?"

"Not much. When I was a kid, an older man lived here, but I didn't see him often. He was very private. When he passed away, the house stayed empty for a while. Then, an older woman moved in. I'd see her sometimes working in the yard, or she'd come late to church, sit in the back row, and leave before anyone else. She had a kind smile but kept her distance. I bet my dad knows more."

"I hope so."

Katherine grinned. "You must have read the journal."

"I did." Elise nodded. "It was written by a young woman named Rosemary, who must have lived here in the 1930s. She was sent to England in 1936 to stay with distant relatives."

"Sounds like there's more to the story than you're telling me."

"I don't want to relate anything that paints Rosemary in a negative light. She was in love with Milton, but he left to make his fortune in New York City, promising he'd send for her."

"They were in love, and he just left her?"

"Can you believe it? I haven't decided if I intensely

dislike Milton or not." How could he leave Rosemary?

Katherine chuckled. "Besides the house project, it sounds like you have something else that will take up your time."

"I am on a mission to discover the rest of Rosemary's story."

"Wasn't there a seller at the closing?"

"No. The documents were electronically signed. Fushia said a company owned the property. Strange that although others made offers on the house, the seller or sellers rejected them."

"So, they were waiting for you."

Elise rubbed the gooseflesh rising on her arms. "That's an interesting and sweet thought." A sense of belonging washed over her. The Victorian had a welcoming presence, as though the old house had been waiting for her.

God had remade her into a new creation, and it was time for this house to get a new makeover.

With a satisfied grin, Richard disconnected the call and leaned back in his office chair. Some of the money he'd saved for years was being put to good use. The wheels of advertising were now in motion.

Soon, his photo and information about his law firm would appear in newspapers, billboards, and social media in every area within a two-hour drive.

Richard Worthington was on his way to success.

Chapter 11

At the chiming of her doorbell, Elise checked her watch. How did it get to be noon?

When she opened her door, she found Chester and his wife, Maybelline, holding pizza boxes on her front porch.

Chester cracked one open, and the delicious aroma drifted toward her. "We thought you might want lunch and help hanging your window blinds and curtains."

"Seriously?" Elise laughed. "You brought lunch and an offer to help?"

"Of course," Maybelline said. "That's what neighbors do for one another. We made sure to bring enough for Katherine and the work crew."

"Wait for me." Henry, carrying two lawn chairs, hurried toward them. "I wasn't sure if you, or someone on the work crew, might need to take a load off your feet. I also have a card table and several other items in my car."

Elise rushed to give him a hand. "Thank you. You are so thoughtful." She couldn't believe they were doing this for her. During her singing days, anyone who visited expected her to provide food, beverages, and entertainment.

In no time, Maybelline covered the little table with the

cute tablecloth she'd brought and arranged the food, paper plates, and plastic utensils. They'd even brought a cooler filled with tea, juice, water, and soft drinks.

Once everyone assembled, Henry led them in a brief prayer, blessing the food, the workers, the house, and Elise.

Tears pricked Elise's eyes, a lump forming in her throat at the unexpected kindness of her new friends. How did she get lucky enough to live in a sweet town like this?

A realization hit her. Her hometown had been like that. Sure, there were a few grumps and gossips, but most people in the community cared deeply for one another. Why hadn't she been more appreciative of what she had?

Maybelline handed Elise a paper plate. "You okay?"

"Yes. Thank you for doing this."

"It's our pleasure. Besides that, I wanted an excuse to tell you what I found about your house and the previous owner."

The thought of discovering some missing information on Rosemary's journey brought a happy jump to Elise's pulse. "I can't wait to hear since I finished the journal last night."

"I hoped you had." Maybelline's eyes sparkled as she directed Elise to the food table. "After lunch, and we help you around the house, would you be willing to share what it said?"

"Definitely." Elise placed pizza on her plate and then chose an ice-cold bottle of soft drink she hadn't had since she was a kid. "I can't wait to fill you in and compare notes."

"Henry can tell you about Mrs. Windsor. She was the previous owner."

Mrs. Windsor? The woman's name surprised Elise. She'd surmised maybe that it would have been Ian's mother. "Wasn't her name Hammond?"

Henry peeked over her shoulder. "No, but there is a connection I think you'll find surprising."

Elise bounced on her toes. "How can I eat and work with all that dangling information waiting to be discovered?"

"I assure you, the feeling is mutual. I barely slept after they called last night and told me you had found a journal."

With a plate piled high with pizza, Chester stood by his wife. "I thought we could share." He gave her a sweet grin, then turned his mischievous gaze toward Elise. "And I can't wait to hear what you tell us about that diary or journal or whatever it is you found."

"I want to know, too." Katherine joined their little circle. "Elise, I hope you don't mind that I let them know your window coverings arrived."

Elise grinned at her new friends. "No worries. It's a blessing to have this much help. How about we meet here at five-thirty to exchange information and compare notes?"

"Would you mind if I call Ian and see if he can join us?" Henry asked.

"Yes, please. Thank you."

The doorbell chimed. Curious about who else might have shown up, Elise hurried to the foyer and opened the door.

In front of her stood the biggest, tallest, most handsome, well-built man she'd ever seen.

"My name is Valentino. I'm here to help."

Elise stood there gaping at the man. An action hero wanted to help her?

She'd seen good-looking guys in California, but Valentino was something else. However, she did notice he wore a wedding ring.

He leaned down as though she hadn't heard him. "Chester said you might need help hanging your blinds." His words had a slight Italian accent.

Elise stepped aside to let him enter. "Please come in."

"Hey, Valentino." Chester shook the big man's massive hand. "Thanks for taking the time to give this little lady a hand."

"My pleasure." Valentino turned to Elise. "My wife, Ursula, works at the medical clinic with Paige, the lady who has the big cat. They both wanted you to know they would love to help with anything you need."

"That's very sweet. Thank you, and please thank them."

"I will do that."

At Valentino's longing glance toward the food table, Elise pointed. "Please help yourself to pizza."

While he placed several slices on his plate, Elise moved to where her friends were finishing their meal. "He is one big man." She whispered to Chester and Maybelline.

"Yep," Chester said. "Valentino is the Eliminator. He had some free time between jobs. Because he's so tall, he's an expert on curtain and blind hanging."

Elise slowly turned to look again at the big man. It's a good thing he eliminated problems and not people.

If only Valentino had been available to help her a few years ago.

Sometimes, two thousand miles didn't seem like enough distance.

Chapter 12

Who knew hanging curtains and blinds could be enjoyable?

Elise hadn't laughed that hard in ages. Maybelline had a couple of one-line zingers that left everyone in stitches. Chester and Henry were a hoot, and even Valentino had a cute sense of humor.

Once Elise's belongings arrived in a few weeks, she could settle into her new home. Maybe she'd buy a blowup mattress and start staying here. But she needed to wait for the security system to be installed. She didn't need to take any chances.

When five-thirty came, her friends assembled in the living room for Elise to share about the journal. Valentino joined them since he was waiting for his wife, who was coming over later to introduce herself. Henry mentioned Ian was running late but should be here soon.

A soft breeze blew through the open windows, fluttering Elise's new curtains as she reviewed her notes.

Careful to honor Rosemary's memory, Elise took her time sharing the basics of what Rosemary had written in her journal. When Elise finished, Maybelline was as heartbroken as Elise over Rosemary's abandonment by Milton and being sent to England to have the baby.

Maybelline wiped her eyes. "How dare Milton take Rosemary's love and leave her to go to New York. He'd pledged his love and promised they would be married many times. If he wanted to make his fortune, he should have married Rosemary and taken her with him. That poor girl."

The rest of the group nodded in agreement.

"I was able to find out a few more details about the house," Maybelline added. "The original owners were Rosemary's parents. Once they passed, their oldest son lived in the house. When he died, a lady named Agatha Windsor came from England and moved in."

Elise pondered the latest information. "I wonder what the connection was with Agatha and Rosemary's family."

Henry raised his hand. "My late wife and I knew Agatha when she lived here. She was very prim and proper and very sweet. Agatha was a widow with very little income, and a relative of Rosemary's family flew her from England to live in the home."

"And I am that relative." Ian walked into their gathering.

A collective gasp rose from the group.

Elise gawked. "You?" Ian Hammond, the gardener, was the relative? "That means that you are..."

"I am Rosemary's great-grandson."

Somewhat shocked by the revelation, Elise handed Ian the journal. "Then this belongs to you."

"Thank you." He cradled the diary, tears welling in his eyes. "I stayed in the other room to listen to what you shared.

Thank you for your kindness about Rosemary and for taking good care of my grandmother's journal."

"After reading what she'd written, it feels like she's a good friend. I'm so sorry she went through the pain of lost love."

"Yes. That is a difficult thing for a heart to bear."

Curious that his comment was more personal than his grandmother's story, Elise gave him a moment to look through the diary. "Would you be willing to answer some questions about her?"

Ian nodded. "I'd be honored."

"Did Rosemary marry and have other children?"

"Yes. She married an older, very kind Englishman who was a widower whose wife had died in childbirth. When he met Rosemary, he fell in love with her and adopted her baby as his own. That baby was my mother."

Elise placed her hand over her heart. "Wow. That's incredible. I'm so relieved and grateful that she found a good man. Do you know if she ever heard from Milton?"

"Before my grandmother passed away, she shared with my mother the truth about her birth father. I don't believe Milton ever contacted Rosemary again. However, she discovered he had married another woman in New York."

"The no-good scoundrel," Chester growled.

"I could have eliminated that problem," Valentino said matter-of-factly.

Elise stifled a nervous giggle at Valentino's statement,

then turned back to Ian. "Did Rosemary ever return to the States?"

"No, she did not," Ian said. "She considered her true home to be in England even as World War II raged around them. Rosemary and her husband sheltered my mother where they lived in the country, giving my mother only happy memories of her childhood. My grandparents were good and loving people."

Elise's lip trembled. "You don't know how relieved this makes me. Rosemary got her happy ending, after all."

"Yes, she did."

"Wait. I'm confused." Chester said. "Rosemary was sent to England, where she met and married an Englishman who adopted her and Milton's baby. And that baby was your mother?"

"Correct."

"So your mother is Rosemary's daughter, which makes you Rosemary's grandson."

"Correct, again."

"Got it." Chester gave him a thumbs-up.

Elise tilted her head. "So, why did a company own this house?"

"The company is mine. When the house came to be in my possession, I was happy and content in England. However, as you know, change happens, and sometimes God places us on another trajectory."

The hairs on the back of Elise's neck shot to attention.

Did Ian know about her past? "Why didn't you move into the big house?"

"I still have an estate in England; therefore, I am happy with smaller quarters. During the five years the house here stayed empty, I prayed and waited to see who God would send." Ian's gentle gaze rested on her. "And thankfully, God sent you."

Elise knew the house was a blessing, but now it seemed a monumental God-given gift. "I promise to take good care of the house for you."

"Take good care of the home for yourself, Elise. Everywhere God sends us, there are God-given gifts along the way and lessons to learn. Use the home for you and for God's glory."

With a sense of holy purpose filling her, Elise met Ian's gaze. "I will."

After everyone left, she closed her windows and locked the front door. Did Ian know about her previous life?

Not wanting to wait to discover the truth, Elise went through the garden and pushed open the iron gate leading to his cottage.

Before she arrived, his door opened. "I thought you might stop by for a chat. Please come in."

Elise couldn't believe the simple beauty inside the little cottage, reminding her of something she'd seen in an old movie. The open floor plan had wood floors, a beamed ceiling, a dark leather couch, and two chairs facing a stone fireplace with bookcases on either side filled with books. Country cottage kitchen cabinets and a wooden table were on the other side of the space. A wall of windows in the back looked out at another small garden. An open door led to a bedroom.

Ian stood beside her. "Do you approve?"

The cottage reminded Elise of something she'd seen in old movies. "It's lovely."

"I designed it after one of my favorite cottages." He motioned to the couch. "Please join me."

Elise settled on the sofa while Ian sat in a chair across from her. "You mentioned you still owned an estate in England. Do you go back often?"

"I do travel quite a bit. My son, his wife, and their children are residents on the property now."

"What keeps you here in Crawdad Beach?"

"Now that you own this home, I will return to England."

She wasn't ready for him to leave. "But it's nice having you here."

Ian's smile was gentle. "I appreciate you think so, but it's time. You have your life, and I will return to mine."

Elise took a breath and let it out slowly. "Do you know who I am?"

"I do. Years ago, during my travels, I stopped by a county fair and heard a beautiful young singer. Although the music was a little loud, the words of the song were captivating. After that, I followed your career and have prayed for you throughout your journey."

Elise's vision swam at the sting of embarrassment for the life she'd led and the surprising warmth of Ian's kindness. "I made a mess of my life."

"God is good about taking messes and making masterpieces."

"I've heard that, but I did the mess part. I'm not sure I will ever be a masterpiece."

"God makes the transformation, and I believe He is doing a wonderful job."

Over the following weeks, Elise worked twice as hard to return the house to its former beauty.

With the help of Katherine and her work crew, Elise's parents, and several sweet townspeople, the house sparkled and shone, almost as though it had straightened its shoulders and could breathe again.

Elise felt the same way. After living in ways that still made her cringe, she could again breathe.

In the late evening, she took her guitar and notebook to the gazebo. Since reading Rosemary's journal and having more conversations with Ian, Elise had an idea for a song about God's love and restoration.

Rosemary had thought her life was over, but God moved her to England to find the man of her dreams and the life she never thought possible.

Two years ago, if someone had told Elise that her career

would end and she'd be happy living in a small town, she would have laughed in their face. But when nodules and polyps formed on her vocal cords, it became impossible for her to sing higher notes. Even surgery couldn't repair the damage.

As her career fell apart, she thought her life had ended. Yet through it all, God had pried away the things that had killed her faith and instead had given her a new and much better life.

As words and a melody took shape, Elise strummed her guitar, looked heavenward, and quietly sang the song that reverberated in her soul.

Chapter 13

Exhilarated, Richard stepped out of the county courthouse and into the hot sunshine. He'd won his first case in his new county. The advertising brought in more business every day, and his firm now showed a nice profit.

He removed his tie and suit jacket. Hopefully, he could get back to Crawdad Beach before Cora left for the day. Though she kept up with her tasks, he noticed her subtle resistance to working late, a quiet defiance in her tired eyes.

If work continued to increase at this pace, he might need to look at hiring a law clerk or paralegal. Yes, life was looking up.

Richard slid into his car and pulled into traffic. Elise's gorgeous face came to mind. He hadn't seen her in weeks, or had it been a month? He didn't have her phone number, so he couldn't call. It was too late to knock on her door when he finished his long workday.

He'd jogged by her house the other night and noticed her roof had been replaced. The front yard was now neatly landscaped, blinds and curtains were in place, and outdoor lighting illuminated the house in a soft and more secure fashion.

Richard hated that he'd missed watching the renovation, and he hated even more that he missed seeing Elise.

Maybe he could carve out a few minutes to stop by her house during his lunch break tomorrow. He shook his head. Not a good plan. His desk was where he ate most of his meals.

He could make time on the weekend. But the stack of documents and cases wouldn't be handled on their own.

How could he work her into his busy schedule? Richard snapped his fingers. He'd have Cora send Elise flowers with a card that contained his phone number and ask her to call him.

Yes, that would work. Then, he could schedule some time to spend with her.

Satisfied he found his answer, Richard turned on the radio and hummed along with the music.

Leaning against her kitchen counter, Elise sipped a glass of sweet iced tea. She couldn't believe the speed with which Katherine had finished the renovation. In California, the permit and inspection process for almost anything took a ridiculous amount of time. The perks of living in Crawdad Beach continued to get better and better.

She'd almost gotten caught up on most of her audio projects in her studio. She enjoyed the renovation, but returning to work felt great.

Elise's phone security app signaled someone had opened

her front gate. She watched as a spiky-blond-haired teenager carried a bouquet of roses in a pretty vase to her door.

Leaving the chain on, she peered through the opening to see what he wanted.

The guy gave her a quick look. "You, Elise Thomas?"

"I am."

"These are for you." He held up the vase.

She unlatched the chain. The guy handed her the flowers, turned, and ran down the sidewalk to his waiting car.

Who would send her a bouquet of red, peach, and pink roses? Elise locked her door and set back the chain. She took a deep whiff of the delightful smell and placed the flowers on her dining room table.

The note read:

Sorry, I've been busy. Call me and let's get together.

Richard.

A work and mobile phone number followed the message.

Richard Worthington wanted her to call him? The roses were beautiful, but seriously? He lived and worked about two minutes away; couldn't he have brought the flowers himself?

Sending them was a thoughtful gesture, and she did love roses. The least she could do was give him a thank-you call.

Should she try his office or personal number? Since he might be busy at work, Elise chose the mobile.

The call went straight to voicemail.

Elise left a nice thank-you message and included her number.

Now she'd wait and see if he was too busy to get back to her.

Richard dropped his briefcase on the coffee table and collapsed on his apartment couch. Business had never been better, and money was flowing into his firm. Why did Cora want to quit?

He leaned forward and rested his head in his hands. He'd offered her more money and a better title and even said he'd hire a receptionist so she could have her own office. But Cora said no, that life was too short to spend every waking moment in an office. At least she'd given him a month's notice to find a replacement.

What was he going to do now? Cora knew just about everyone in town and had knowledge that would put other lawyers to shame.

He'd probably have to hire three people to do the work she did. How could he afford to do that? His profits would fly out the window.

Richard shifted his perspective. If he pushed himself, he could have a big staff and take on even more clients.

Cora would be with him for another month. During that time, he'd have her help him interview her replacement.

Maybe he could hire a recent high school grad as his receptionist who'd work for minimum wage. Then, if he needed to add another person, He could make it work.

Richard's stomach growled and rumbled. Did he eat dinner? He checked his watch as he walked to his kitchen.

How could it be one o'clock in the morning? No wonder Cora was upset with him. If he begged her again to stay and promised she could leave during regular working hours, maybe she'd change her mind.

He opened his refrigerator and stared at what little was inside — an apple, a bunch of grapes that looked more like raisins, two bottles of water, and a piece of fried chicken he'd brought home from Tiddlywinks a few days ago. He sniffed the meat. It seemed good enough.

Richard sat at his kitchen table and scrolled through his phone as he munched his meal.

Rats! He missed Elise's phone call. Well, too late now. At least he had her number. Tomorrow morning, if he had time, he'd call her.

Wait. Surely, he had time to make one small phone call.

Didn't he?

Maybe Cora was right that he was working too hard. But how could he succeed if he didn't stretch himself?

Then again, how far would he stretch before he was in danger of breaking?

Chapter 14

Twenty days. His secretary/paralegal/all-around amazing helper was leaving in twenty days. Richard blew out a breath. Nothing he offered to Cora had changed her mind.

The long hours he had her working were only part of the problem. Cora wanted to spend her golden years with her husband, exploring the world instead of being in an office.

Richard took off his glasses and rubbed the bridge of his nose. How would he make it without Cora? He'd come into the office at five thirty this morning and barely made a dent in all that needed to be done.

Why did he pay so much money for advertisements? He should have been more patient and slowly built his practice.

He put back on his glasses and stared at the clock on the wall across from him. How did it get to be so late in the day? He'd forgotten to eat lunch again; it was already time for dinner.

The silent, ticking clock felt like a bomb about to explode, scattering the shrapnel of his failures.

Based on the time he'd spent busting his tail to build his business, the firm's profit had increased, but what had it gotten him?

Richard pushed away from his desk and strode out of his office.

With a glance in his direction, Cora pulled her purse from the bottom desk drawer. “I’ll see you in the morning.”

Why did she have to leave at five thirty? Couldn’t she stay as late as he did? Richard forced a smile. “See you then.”

Cora turned toward him. “Richard, you don’t have to work so hard. Carlton built up a nice practice working from nine to five.”

He gave Cora a brisk nod. “Thanks for the advice.”

She patted his arm. “Why not visit the woman you sent those flowers to?”

Richard’s hand flew to his forehead. He’d forgotten to call Elise. For several days, he’d forgotten to call her. “I need to do that.” He took a breath and blew it out. “Cora, thank you for all you do for me and the practice.”

“You’re welcome. And don’t worry, we’ll find a replacement before I leave. See you in the morning.”

“See you.” Richard took off his tie as he watched her leave. The advertisement to replace Cora he’d put in online job sites had netted interest, but no one he would consider hiring.

What was he going to do?

Richard pulled up his sagging pants. He kept forgetting to eat. He was exhausted and barely slept. Would becoming the most successful lawyer in the world make him happy and content? Based on the last few weeks, no.

Plus, he'd been so busy he'd forgotten to call the beautiful woman he wanted to get to know better.

What did he really want out of life?

He shrugged off his jacket, locked his office, and headed to his apartment.

He needed to figure out who he was and what he wanted.

Elise stopped in the foyer after showing Paige and her big cat around her house. "So, what do you think?"

"It's gorgeous." Paige and Sir Purrcevel stopped next to her. "I appreciate you giving us a tour. Since Quinn's out running errands, Sir Purrcevel and I were curious to see how your renovation was progressing."

The big cat meowed as though he agreed with her statement.

"Thank you." Elise grinned as she rubbed Sir Purrcevel's back. "I'm glad you both like and approve of the house."

Since Elise met Paige on the sidewalk the first week in Crawdad Beach, they'd become good friends. Friday night pizza and game night at Paige and Quinn's house had become something she looked forward to every week. She wasn't very good at card or board games, but she did have a great time with the couple and the other townspeople who joined for the fun.

"Did you hire a decorator for your house?" Paige asked.

"No, not here. I just used the furniture and accessories that I already had."

"I'm impressed. Your home should be featured in a magazine."

Elise held up her hands. "No, I'd prefer to stay in the background."

"Well, everything is beautiful. I still can't believe you have a recording studio. I wouldn't have a clue what to do with all that equipment. Thank you for giving me a list of the audiobooks you narrated. When I get home, I'll order a few."

"I hope you enjoy the stories. It's fun to be a voice for their characters."

"That would be enjoyable." Paige hugged Elise. "Thanks again for letting us stop by."

Elise's phone security app signaled someone had opened the front gate.

Paige peeked over her shoulder. "Your security system includes cameras and notifications? I'm impressed."

"I got a great deal on the service." Elise acted like it wasn't a big deal. She didn't need to explain why the property was so heavily secured. She could not take chances after what happened in California.

At the chime of the doorbell, Paige grinned. "Maybe that's Quinn now."

"Not Quinn. It's our new town lawyer, Richard Worthington."

"Really? I heard he's rather handsome." Paige wiggled her

eyebrows. "And isn't he the one who sent you the flowers?"

"He is cute, and yes, he sent the flowers last week." Elise glanced at the flowers still sitting on her dining room table.

"We'd better go so you two can be alone. Come on, Sir Purrcevel, Quinn's probably wondering what happened to us. Don't forget we have another game night on Friday."

"I'll be there. But I warn you, I plan to win this time."

When Elise opened the door, Sir Purrcevel hunched down in stalking mode and moved toward him.

Richard's eyebrows raised to his hairline as he stood still. "Does your furry mountain lion bite?" He whispered through clenched teeth.

Knowing that Sir Purrcevel was harmless, Elise raised her shoulders. "I'm not sure. Paige, does he bite?"

Paige chuckled and reached for the ornery feline. "Not too much. Just stay super still. Sir Purrcevel, you need to behave."

The cat's meow sounded like a muffled laugh as he rubbed against Richard's pant leg.

"I think he likes you." Elise grinned.

Richard stayed in a rigid position. "He's probably sizing me up to eat me when you turn your backs."

"Excuse my manners. Richard Worthington, this is Paige Young. She works at the medical clinic."

"Nice to meet you." His eyes flicked toward Paige, then back to the cat.

"Nice to meet you, too." Paige snapped the leash on the

big cat's harness. "We'd better go. Enjoy your evening."

Sir Purrcevel's tail wound around Richard's leg, then jerked with a quick whip as he sauntered off with his mistress.

Richard's mouth dropped open. "That mountain lion just tail-whipped me."

Elise laughed at his incredulous stare. "Sir Purrcevel is known to be quite the character. He's one of those Maine cats crossed with a Persian variety, and who knows what."

"Whatever he is, he is one big feline."

"He is quite humongous." Elise agreed as she surveyed Richard. He was a handsome man, and he looked nice in his polo shirt and jeans.

He cleared his throat.

Heat rose on the back of her neck. How long had she just been staring at him? "Oh. I'm sorry. Won't you come in?"

He hesitated. "You don't have any other animals in there, do you?"

"No, not unless you count a teddy bear I've had since I was a kid. I'm pretty sure he doesn't bite."

"I came to apologize for not getting back to you sooner."

Elise motioned him to follow her to the living room. "No apology is necessary. I'm sure you've been busy. Thank you very much for the beautiful flowers."

"You're welcome." He rubbed the back of his neck as he sat on the opposite end of the couch. "I've been busy. Way too busy. I've been meaning to stop by sooner. I'm sorry about that. Time keeps getting away from me." His quiet words, barely a whisper, as though thinking out loud rather than talking to her.

Elise playfully wagged a finger at him. "Just don't turn into a Milton, okay?"

"Excuse me?" A confused expression clouded Richard's face. "I don't know who you're talking about."

"I'm sorry. That's right. You weren't here when I shared about the journal we found in the house. Rosemary, a young woman in the 1930s, hid her diary under a floorboard in the attic. She'd fallen in love with a guy named Milton, and he seemed to love her too. But he left Rosemary to make his fortune in New York. I know you're busy, but please don't be like Milton and allow money and success to be your driving force."

She knew that truth all too well. When a talent scout spotted her singing at a county fair, he offered to represent her if she would come to Los Angeles. Elise had been a high school graduate who thought she knew everything. Against her family's wishes, she ditched college, grabbed her savings, loaded her car, and headed for California.

Richard's brow furrowed as he stared at her. "I will try not to be a Milton."

Elise refocused on him. "Good."

He shifted and gazed around the room before looking again at her. "So, how have you been?"

"Good. You?"

"Busy."

At the awkward exchange, Elise couldn't help but smile. "Want a tour of the house?"

"Yes. I'd love to see the remodel." Richard quickly stood and held his hand out toward her.

She accepted his help. He pulled her gently to her feet and kept her hand in his. They stood facing each other. His gaze locked with hers, and a blush crept up her neck, warming her cheeks.

Warmth and vulnerability flashed in Richard's eyes for a moment. He released her hand and stepped back. "Lead the way."

Elise could sense his gaze on her back as she directed him to the other room.

Just who was Richard Worthington? He seemed arrogant and driven at his office. Yet, being around him now, she noted a touch of insecurity or something she couldn't quite decipher. Whatever it was, she wouldn't mind taking the time to discover more about the handsome lawyer.

Chapter 15

Richard needed to be careful and not drawn in by his attraction to Elise. He'd made that mistake before with Annie, and that only left him with a messed-up heart.

He followed Elise up the stairs as she gave him a tour of her home. "You mentioned you found a journal. Did you find anything else, like a hidden room?"

Elise paused. "No, I don't think the house has any."

"My great-grandparents had a hidden nook behind a bookcase. My brother and I won hide and seek every year since we didn't tell our cousins about it."

She raised an eyebrow as her blue-gray eyes surveyed him. "That doesn't sound fair."

"It wasn't." Richard grinned. "But we did eventually tell them."

"When you were adults?" Elise deadpanned.

He attempted a wounded look. "No. We were much younger than that. I was a freshman in college."

She hiked an eyebrow. "Sounds like you and your brother were mischievous."

"My younger brother is the ringleader. He's a risk-taker and more outgoing." Richard grimaced. Why was he telling

Elise about his brother?

"You're a lawyer." Elise cocked her head. "Don't you have to be outgoing?"

"Working with clients is different."

Elise's grin took a mischievous turn. "Because you control the narrative and can even charge for the time."

"I probably should be offended by that statement."

"No offense was meant. Just an observation."

He shouldn't ask, but he was curious. "What else do you observe?"

Elise, still grinning, stepped back. Her gaze roamed from his head to his toes, making heat rise on the back of his neck.

"I see a lawyer who probably shouldn't ask questions he might not want answered."

Richard grinned back at her. "That bad, huh?"

"No. Nothing bad. I see a handsome man who longs to be successful. Success is desirable, but it often comes at a cost."

He forced himself not to react to her perceptiveness. "Do you speak from experience?"

Elise's grin dimmed. "Unfortunately, yes. Fame and fortune are a double-edged sword that can leave deep cuts." She turned away and hurried through the upstairs, momentarily pausing at the guest rooms and office. She briefly opened a door at the end of the hallway.

He peeked inside before she closed it. "Why do you have a recording studio?"

She shrugged. "I'm the voice behind some audiobooks, a

few commercials, and I also dabble in a few other recording projects."

Richard studied her for a moment. Her tall, slender body and fascinating eyes made the pieces fall into place. She no longer wore wild makeup, had spiky short hair, and used a weird stage name. Elise Thomas had been famous.

He leaned against the doorframe. "There's more to you than you're telling me."

Elise hoped her face didn't show a reaction to Richard's question. Had he recognized her? Why did she show him her studio?

Without responding to Richard's inquiry, she turned and walked away, motioning for him to follow. "I've saved the best for last."

He caught up. "You didn't answer my question."

She went through the kitchen and out the back door. "What do you think?"

Richard stood beside her. "About you not answering my question or your beautiful garden?"

Might as well get it over with. Elise took a deep breath and met his gaze. "What do you want to know?"

"Why you gave up a successful singing career and moved to Crawdad Beach." Richard didn't sound rude, just curious.

"Why do you think I gave up anything?"

"You were a rock star." Richard's voice held a level of awe. "You're much prettier now without all the makeup, crazy outfits, and short, spiky hair. The recording studio helped put the pieces together. Why did you give it up?"

Elise crossed her arms, wishing she could erase that part of her life. "I'm not that person anymore. Besides, I didn't give up anything. I gained everything."

His brows furrowed. "That doesn't make sense. Who wouldn't want to be famous?"

"I thought that, too, until it happened." She looked away. "You don't want to know about my previous life."

"Try me. I'm a good listener."

"Why?" Elise scoffed. "So you can post it on social media that you found me?"

Richard seemed genuinely surprised. "Why would I do that?"

She pinched her eyes shut. "It's happened before," Elise whispered.

Elise found out the hard way that not everyone who wanted to get close to her did so because they cared and had her best interests at heart.

She'd been way too trusting in the past. People used her to make themselves look important or to get an inroad into the recording industry; the terrible thing is, she'd done the same thing.

Richard lightly touched her arm. "Hey, I'm sorry. I didn't mean to make you uncomfortable. I was just curious and wanted to get to know you better."

Maybe she'd give him the benefit of the doubt. "Want to sit in the gazebo?"

He hesitated for a moment, then nodded. "If you're sure, you're okay with me being here. We don't have to talk about anything you don't want to discuss."

"It's a nice evening. We can talk."

"I appreciate you trusting me." A tenderness in Richard's eyes held her steady.

She strolled along the pathway to the gazebo, turned on the ceiling fan, and sat in one of her wicker chairs.

His gaze traveled around the area as he settled next to her. "Your gardens are incredible."

"I can't take credit. They were already like this when I bought the house."

"I thought the house had been empty for a few years?"

"It had. But Ian Hammond, the gardener, stays in the cottage." Elise pointed to the back gate.

Richard's eyebrows drew together. "Why would he do that?"

"Ian was actually the property owner."

"I thought a company owned the house."

"The company is Ian's."

"Interesting. I'm sure there is more to that story, but I'd like to know more about you, the real Elise Thomas. Not to post anything on social media." At Richard's cute smile, a dimple on his cheek made him look even more appealing.

Was she making a mistake trusting Richard? She barely knew him, yet here they were in her gazebo. Maybe, just maybe, it would be okay to let him get closer. At least, she hoped so. Because she sensed Richard Worthington might need a trustworthy friend even more than she did.

Chapter 16

Why had she done that?

Elise kept trying to focus on making her recording but couldn't concentrate.

Spending the evening with Richard had been wonderful. Too wonderful. They'd sat in her gazebo for hours, and she'd revealed her past, including her highs and lows and her many failures. She'd just blurted it out and kept sharing as though they'd been friends for years.

No one knew, not even her family, about some things she'd told Richard.

Argh! Ack!

Why?

Why had she been so trusting? This morning, Richard could call one of those celebrity tell-all magazines and give them the scoop of the century.

Elise steadied her breathing. Maybe everything would be fine. Maybe Richard really was trustworthy. Hopefully, he'd keep the attorney-client privilege and not share anything his client told him.

But she wasn't his client.

Elise ran her hands through her hair. She needed to get

outside.

Warm, humid air blanketed Elise's skin as she stepped onto the back porch. She took her time strolling along the pathway leading to the gazebo. The sweet scent of blooming flowers calmed her nerves. Spotting something inside one rose, she leaned closer.

A bee was lying on one petal.

Was he hurt? She gently touched the flower, and the bee stumbled as if just waking up.

Elise puffed out a laugh. She'd seen photos of bees napping, their fuzzy bodies nestled among flower petals, but never seen one herself until now.

Had the bee been so busy that he dropped from exhaustion? She'd done that more times than she could count during her touring days.

The little bee gathered more pollen and flew away.

"Good morning!" Ian, holding a bucket and gardening tools, stood at the garden gate. "Mind if I come inside?"

"Please do. I just saw the cutest thing. A little bee had fallen asleep in one of the roses."

Ian grinned as he came toward her. "That is quite a find. Although I've heard that can happen, I haven't had that pleasure." He set down his tools. "How are you today?"

"Good. Kinda." Or at least she hoped everything would be okay with Richard. Why had she talked so freely with him?

"Need a listening ear?"

"I think I've already talked too much."

Ian picked up his garden implements. "Then I will not bother you and come back at another time."

"No, please stay." Elise always enjoyed talking to Ian. "I was just paranoid about sharing some of my past with our town's lawyer."

"Richard Worthington? He seems like a nice young man."

"You've met him?"

Ian stooped to remove a dead stem from a plant. "Not personally."

Elise moved next to him. "So you've heard things?"

"I've heard Richard is desirous of success, but his heart is good. I'm friends with the previous town's lawyer, Carlton McGee."

"Oh. So, Richard is a nice guy?" She hated that her voice sounded needy, but she wanted to find out who he really was.

"Carlton would not leave his firm to anyone he didn't believe would be a good fit for Crawdad Beach. He has high hopes for Richard." Ian straightened and gazed at her. "With your previous career, I'm sure you are cautious when it comes to getting close to people."

"I've been burned more times than I can count by those who I thought were my friends and I thought I could trust. I was so naïve when I started in the music industry, which led to heartache, heartbreak, and a very scary situation. It wasn't just what other people did. It's what I did. I screwed up in so many ways." How she wished she could go back in time and do so many things differently.

"Everyone has had failures, even those we Christians call heroes of the faith. The Bible clearly shows that no one is perfect besides Jesus Christ, the Son of God." Ian's kind voice was reassuring. "God is forgiving, and He uses imperfect people for His perfect plans."

"I'm so grateful for His forgiveness."

"As am I. Consider giving yourself grace and trusting God for your past and future."

Elise rubbed her arms. "I know I should, but I told Richard some things I hadn't shared with anyone before." She cringed at the ridiculous honesty of telling him about her many failures, inappropriate relationships, and bad choices.

Ian's tender gaze met hers. "Perhaps it was time." He removed a spent flower and gave it to her. "Inside the withered petals, tiny seeds hold potential for new life. While we can't alter what's happened in our past, each experience, no matter how positive or negative, provides lessons and growth that shape our future."

Elise held the faded and dry flower in her hand. She'd already asked God for forgiveness for the many things she'd done wrong. He'd picked her up out of the slimy pit of her past and given her a fresh start.

She needed to learn from her mistakes, stop worrying about what she couldn't change, and enjoy the new life God had given her.

What was he thinking?

Richard took off his glasses and stared sightlessly at the paperwork before him.

Why did he tell Elise what drove his desire for success and his difficulties with his father? His dad always wanted his firstborn son to do more, be better, and make something of himself. To please his father, Richard abandoned his dream of playing basketball and pursued a career in law. Not only had he shared that with Elise, but he'd also told her about what happened with Annie.

A throbbing headache tightened its grip. Richard rubbed his temples, trying to ease the pressure.

Why had he been so comfortable with Elise? They barely knew one another. Yet when she shared her story, he willingly shared his.

Why?

Spending the evening with Elise had been peaceful, comfortable, and relaxing. How long had it been since he'd felt that way?

There had been an undercurrent of unease with Annie, his brain sending warning signals he'd ignored.

Richard put back on his glasses and tried to concentrate on his work. But he couldn't focus. The memory of sitting with Elise brought back a feeling of tranquility he desperately wanted to recapture

Why did he think a hectic pace would be an answer to

the restlessness of his soul?

Why couldn't he go back and start his life over? Richard stood and peered out the front window. If only he could time-travel to go back to change his life and his choices. He'd even want to return to when he first arrived in Crawdad Beach and take life slower.

Hoping it wasn't too late, Richard asked Cora if she'd step into his office.

As she stood in front of his desk, he closed the door.

He faced Cora. "I'm sorry. I'm sorry I pushed you so hard. I want to do a restart. Would you be willing to help me?"

A small smile touched the corners of her mouth. "I would love to help you with a restart."

"I'm going to cancel all advertisements, finish the cases we've agreed to take, and be more diligent to only pursue what is appropriate for a small law office."

"Richard Worthington, I'm proud of you."

Hearing those words made him stand a little taller. "Thank you."

"Why don't you ask Carlton to assist you with some of these cases you've taken until you get out from under the pressure?"

"You think he'd do that?"

"I know he would be thrilled."

Richard grimaced. What if Carlton said something to Richard's father that he needed help? What if his dad thought he was a failure?

Eyes full of compassion, Cora leaned toward him. "Carlton is a man of character who will not share anything you do not want to be shared, including your family."

Was he that easy to read? Richard breathed a sigh of relief, the knot in his stomach unwinding. "Thank you. I appreciate knowing that."

"Anything else I can help you with?"

"No, that's all. Thanks.

"Richard, God has good things for you here. Don't miss what He's given."

Richard waited until Cora left and looked at the ceiling.

Was that true?

Did God have good things for him?

He was so tired of trying to please his dad, make enough money, and have enough success that Annie would regret leaving him.

What had that gotten him?

Nothing but stressed out and miserable.

It was time to appreciate what he had instead of always pushing for more. His dad might not like it, but Richard needed to decide what *he* wanted out of life.

The first step was to reconnect with God.

Chapter 17

Thank goodness her friend Paige worked at the Crawdad Beach medical clinic. Elise sat on the examination table and tried not to whimper while waiting for her X-ray results.

She couldn't believe she'd slipped and twisted her ankle. At least it was on her left leg, so she could still drive. But what if it was broken? Her main bedroom and kitchen were on the main level, but how would she get upstairs to her recording studio and office?

"X-ray didn't show any breaks," Paige said as she entered the room.

Elise blew out a relieved breath. "That's good news."

"Yes. We'll get your ankle wrapped tight. Then I want you to take care of yourself and remember the RICE method."

"As in eating rice?"

"No." Paige chuckled. "R is for rest. I is for ice. C is for compression, and E is for elevate. So today, rest, use ice to reduce swelling, keep the ankle in a compression bandage, and elevate your foot. Tomorrow, I want you to start very gently stretching your ankle. Don't overextend or do too much. Stretching will help blood circulation and aid in healing."

Paige wrapped Elise's ankle. "I'll send you home with a pair of crutches. Since you live in a two-story house, do you need help with anything?"

"No, I'll be fine." Elise grimaced as the wrap tightened. "It just puts a damper on what I wanted to do this afternoon."

"Are you working on more audiobooks?"

"I was hoping to record a song I've written."

Paige's head popped up. "I'd love to hear it sometime."

"It's only a demo to send to an artist friend so she can make a recording to release the song."

"You wouldn't want to do it yourself?" Paige finished tending to the ankle and stepped back.

"My voice doesn't carry high notes very well." Elise avoided Paige's curious gaze. Why did she tell her that sad fact?

"Is that why you stopped your singing career?"

Elise's stomach dropped. "You know?"

"Of course. Several people in town recognized you."

"But I wanted to hide from the world." What would she do now? Would she need to move and start over somewhere else? Why couldn't she live a quiet life?

Paige laid a hand on Elise's shoulder. "Don't worry. Your secret is safe."

"How can it be if the whole town knows?"

"I didn't say everyone knows." A kind grin graced Paige's face. "Don't worry. You'd be surprised at the ability of Crawdadians to guard their own. We also have several people in town who have experience in security if you ever need help."

A disturbing thought crossed Elise's mind.

Had she shared her secrets with someone who would blab to others?

Why had she trusted Richard? It hadn't even been twenty-four hours, and he'd already told people.

Elise crossed her arms. "Did Richard tell you who I was?"

"Richard? The lawyer?" Paige shook her head. "No. I don't talk to him."

"Did he tell other people?" Elise got off the exam table and grimaced as her throbbing ankle hit the floor. She knew it. She never should have trusted another man.

"I haven't talked to Richard, and I haven't heard that he's talked to anyone else. He seems like a decent guy and is a private person. I hardly ever see him around town."

Elise took in a shuddering breath. Okay, so maybe Richard didn't tell anyone. Even so, she didn't want other people to know who she was.

"I figured out who you were pretty quickly," Paige said. "You look different from your rockstar days, without the crazy makeup, clothes, and short spiky hair, but it still wasn't hard to figure out."

"What am I going to do now?"

"I hope you'll stay here and trust us."

"You don't understand," Elise whispered, her voice thick with unshed tears.

Paige gently hugged her. "I don't know all you've been through, but I know the dangers of trusting people. You'd be surprised how many people in this little town have found a shelter and safe place here."

Elise took in a steadying breath. She believed God brought her to Crawdad Beach, so she needed to trust Him to care for her.

Richard spent time in prayer, asking God to help him get his priorities straight. He couldn't undo his past with Annie. The further away from that relationship, the more apparent it became that her affections had been superficial. She never really loved him.

As for his job, he could strive to work in excellence, but he didn't need to please a woman, his dad, or anyone else but God.

Richard held the takeout food sacks in one hand as he opened Elise's unlocked gate. After his confessions about his past, he hoped she'd want to see him again.

Earlier today, when he looked out from his office window, he'd seen her hobbling along on a pair of crutches to her car. He would have run to her aid if he hadn't been so busy. Thankfully, with Carlton's help, the workload was becoming more manageable.

Richard rang Elise's doorbell and waited. From inside, he

could hear the thump of her crutches coming closer.

A soft click preceded the door opening, and Elise greeted him with a smile.

"I hope you don't mind and haven't eaten yet. I brought dinner from Tiddlywinks."

"That's so sweet. Thank you." Elise maneuvered to the side to allow him to enter. "Will you join me?"

"I was hoping you'd say that. What happened to your foot?" He closed the door and followed her slow progress to the kitchen.

"I twisted my ankle."

"Ouch. That's painful. I'm sorry. But you could have told me something more dramatic. Like you were pole vaulting in the backyard."

Elise chuckled. "I'll have to work on my stories."

"Please have a seat and let me serve you." Richard helped Elise settle at her kitchen table and pulled a chair up for her to rest her foot. "But first, you'll need to direct me to your plates and silverware." Following her directions, he got the items for the meal and sat across from her.

With her eyes closed, Elise prayed a heartfelt prayer, blessing the food, their time together, and for his well-being.

How long had it been since he was with a woman, other than his mother, who prayed? Richard swallowed the burn pressing at the back of his throat.

When she finished praying, he placed his napkin on his lap and met her gaze. "Thanks for praying. I should have been praying for you and your ankle. I promise to do better and keep you in my prayers."

Tears welled in Elise's eyes. "Thanks. I can use all that I can get. I'm glad you're here."

"Thanks for letting me stay." His gaze held hers a second too long before he turned his attention to the food in front of him.

The fact that Elise was glad he'd come to visit made Richard sit a little straighter in his chair.

And if all went well, maybe she'd agree they could see much more of one another.

Chapter 18

“**I** can’t believe you beat me,” Richard grumbled as they left game night.

Elise giggled at his playful tone. “Man up, lawyer man. Did you think you could have won at charades when the category was song titles?”

“I can’t sing, but I know music. How do you think I figured out who you were? ”

The chirping of crickets floated on the evening breeze. Frogs joined in the night song, bringing a bass tone.

She gave Richard a questioning look. “Did you used to listen to my music? I didn’t take you for a rocker kind of guy.”

“I can rock out with the best of them.” He pretended to play an air guitar, his eyes closed and a grin spreading across his face as he rocked back and forth.

Elise laughed. “I’m impressed.”

“Don’t be. I enjoy music but have absolutely no skill at singing or playing a real instrument.” He opened the passenger side door of his car for her and helped her inside.

She had been more than happy to have him chauffeur her back and forth since she was still trying not to overuse her sore ankle.

Elise grinned up at him. "Besides the last category where I beat you, you rocked at game playing."

"Thanks. Overall, I guess I did pretty well." Richard hurried around and sat in the driver's seat. "Playing against you guys was intimidating with Valentino on your team."

"He probably gave us an advantage. It was funny that his wife, Ursula, was the most aggressive player. She's so soft-spoken and sweet until her turn. And Chester and Maybelline cracked me up. Who would have thought someone as old as our grandparents would be great at games?"

"Your team didn't just have the Valentino advantage. Sir Purrcevel was eyeing me like he'd attack at any moment."

"I did notice the big cat seemed to take an unusual interest in you. Are you not a cat lover?"

"Animals of the feline variety are fine. However, I'm more of a dog person."

"Maybe Sir Purrcevel sensed that about you. Since he was sitting on our side of the room, he was probably just being competitive."

"Just try playing with a group of lawyers," Richard said. "My dad, brother, and I are all in the profession. Games aren't just games. They are all-out competitions."

"I can't imagine. My parents remind me of the old cartoon with the little chipmunks, Chip and Dale, who were always super nice to one another. Mom and Dad are overly polite and never want anyone to lose. I can't tell you how many games would end in a tie."

"Well, you didn't seem to have any problems beating our team." Richard stopped at the iron gate guarding her driveway and waited.

Elise clicked the link to let them inside. "We won, but I'm sure you noticed I was very polite as I gloated over our win."

He grinned as he stopped the car by her side entrance. "I believe polite gloating is a contradiction in terms."

Elise waited until Richard came to help.

He opened the door and held out his hand. "May I escort you into your beautiful home?" Richard's firm grip brought her to her feet, and she stood before him. His gaze moved from her eyes and lingered on her lips.

Elise's cheeks heated as she tried not to smile, lick her lips, or lean closer.

His gaze met hers. "Would you mind?"

"If you're asking what I think you're asking. I would not mind at all."

He laid his lips on hers, the kiss gentle.

Richard initiated the contact, but Elise prolonged it.

When their lips parted, he looked down at her and smiled. "Nice."

Elise fanned her face. "More than nice. Thank you, counselor. For a lawyer, you're a good kisser."

His eyebrows shot up. "For a lawyer?"

She laughed at his perplexed expression. "Just teasing. You're a great kisser, but maybe we need more practice." Elise attempted to look innocent.

Richard grinned and kissed her again. "I am at your service anytime you want to continue practicing."

"You are a most kind gentleman."

"Not sure about that. I'd better get you safely inside before you think otherwise."

A car passed on the street, the sound of one of Elise's old songs playing on the radio.

Richard grinned. "For a famous person, you're a great kisser. I'll see you soon."

A rumble of thunder came in the distance as Elise watched Richard pull away. Strange. She didn't think the forecast called for rain. Maybe there was a storm on the coast.

Elise locked her door, set the alarm, and hobbled to her bedroom. Game night with Richard had been wonderful. She loved his cute sense of humor and his easy interaction with her other friends. He seemed more at ease and not in such a hurry. Maybe he was finally embracing the joys of small-town living and not pushing so hard to be what others termed successful.

She loved the town, her house, and the garden. And she enjoyed getting to know the very handsome lawyer who was a great kisser.

A few years ago, she thought her life was over. But God had blessed her in more ways than she could count.

Elise washed her face, put on her comfortable pajamas, and turned down her comforter.

Did she remember to shut her driveway gate?

Elise checked her security app, and sure enough, the gate was wide open. Thank goodness she lived in a safe town. She pressed the link to ensure the gate was closed, then turned on her alarm system.

Satisfied that everything was secure, Elise put on her robe and limped toward the kitchen. Her ankle was throbbing after all the activity.

Without turning on the light, she filled a glass with water from her refrigerator. Elise leaned against the counter, gazing out the back window.

A movement in the shadows drew Elise's attention. Her throat closing, she backed away from the window.

Oh, God. Please no.

Had he found her again?

Chapter 19

Blood whooshing in her ears, Elise hurried as fast as she could on her sore ankle.

Safe in her bedroom, she locked the door and scanned the cameras connected to her phone's security app. All the windows, doors, and gates were securely locked.

She checked each camera's view on her phone but didn't see anything. Maybe it had only the wind moving the trees, causing a shadow. Elise took her laptop from her nightstand and double-checked each camera angle.

Everything looked still.

Elise took a deep breath and tried to calm down. Surely, it was all her imagination. She didn't need to be paranoid.

Did she?

She took her pistol out of her nightstand drawer. Her mom made her promise to stop sleeping with the gun under her pillow. Fortunately, she knew how to use the weapon and was an excellent marksman.

Growing up in the country gave me plenty of opportunities for target practice. She'd never want to use a gun against a person, but she didn't want to take any chances. Rolf Bitler had told her that if he couldn't have her, then no one would.

Rolf had gone from being a fan of hers and attending every concert to a creepy, relentless stalker. He wasn't a big man, but his dark eyes, brown shoulder-length hair, and beard gave him a wolf-like appearance.

An ice-like shiver ran down Elise's spine.

She'd filed a restraining order against Rolf two years ago, but since that was in California, would it apply in South Carolina? She'd hired security during that time, but now, who would she call if she needed help?

Elise checked the backyard and side cameras to view Ian's cottage. His car was gone, so he must not be home. Which meant if someone had been out there, it was not the gardener.

She needed to think. No, she needed to pray for protection, guidance, and wisdom. She believed God had brought her to Crawdad Beach; therefore, shouldn't things go smoothly?

Elise shook her head. That was not a valid point because, in the Biblical account of God leading the Israelites to the promised land, they faced many battles and hardships. Shadrach, Meshach, and Abednego's devotion to God did not prevent their being thrown into a fiery furnace. Even faithful Daniel was placed in a hungry lion's den because he prayed to God.

Thankfully, God showed up in each of those cases with divine protection. But she knew God's blessings often come with difficulties and hardship.

Elise sank to her knees by her bed and prayed.

Much calmer after her prayer time, she rose to her feet and rechecked the view from each camera. All seemed quiet.

Leaving her bedroom door locked, Elise placed her pistol under the pillow beside hers, crawled into bed, and turned off the lamp on her nightstand.

Tomorrow, she needed to be honest with a few trusted people in town about her stalker. Valentino would be first on her list. From what she'd heard from Chester and Maybelline, he was the one to call if you needed help. Hopefully, he'd be open to helping her eliminate her problem.

Morning light filtered through her curtains. Elise groaned and forced open her eyes. Was it morning already? Between staring at the ceiling, listening to every creak of the old house, and having nightmares, she'd barely got any sleep.

Elise trudged to the bathroom and took a quick shower. Maybe she should get a big dog, a massive one who loved her and would attack anyone who dared to bother her. Or she could ask Paige to have Sir Purrcevel stay with her at night. Elise chuckled at the thought of the big cat stalking out of the darkness after whoever dared to enter her domain.

A few hours later, Valentino came over, and Elise explained about her stalker. Thankfully, Valentino agreed to help. He advised her to register her existing restraining order with local authorities since she was in a new state. He also mentioned he had friends in town who were cybersecurity specialists who would help track Rolf.

By five in the afternoon, Elise had registered her restraining order with the local police but barely made any headway on her latest project.

She sat in her studio and attempted to make a recording for the third time. The book she was reading to make an audible version was great, but she was having trouble concentrating.

Worrying about Rolf and wondering what would happen with Richard kept Elise's brain working on overdrive. She'd made too many mistakes in her past and dated men she should have avoided. She did not want to get involved with anyone until she made sure they were spiritually on the same page.

Checking her phone, Elise noticed Richard had left her a message. He wanted to take her to a casual dinner and a walk on the beach.

Getting out of the house this evening would be nice. She enjoyed being with Richard, and being with him again would give her an opportunity to find out where he stood.

Richard stayed close to Elise as they strolled along the beach. She held her sandals in her slender fingers. Her sundress swayed in time with her steps.

A seagull, its wings catching the last rays of the setting

sun, silently glided in the evening air.

The area wasn't empty of people, yet quiet. There were no rowdy beachgoers, just a few people strolling along the sand, sitting quietly in their beach chairs, or standing in the waves near the shoreline.

Although they'd enjoyed a pleasant conversation during the meal, Elise seemed distracted. Richard blew out a breath. Maybe he shouldn't have kissed her last night. "Was your food okay?"

The breeze swirled Elise's blonde hair as her gaze met his. "Dinner was great. Thank you."

"Is something bothering you?"

She continued walking, then stopped. "Yes, I'm sorry." Her gaze dropped to the sand at her feet.

Tension crawled up Richard's neck. Was their relationship over before it barely started?

"I need to tell you something." Her voice was quiet as she gazed up at him.

He wanted to take her hand and not let her go. Instead, he shoved his hands in his back shorts pockets.

A glossy sheen spread over Elise's eyes. "I told you some things about my past, but not everything."

"You don't have to tell me anything."

"No, I do." She stepped into the ocean. Gentle waves lapped at her ankles. "There's a guy."

Richard internally groaned. Elise had a boyfriend. He knew it was too good to be true. A beauty like Elise wouldn't be alone. He waded into the water, stood beside her, and waited.

"A man," Elise took a quivering breath, "has been stalking me for a few years. Last night, after you left, I saw something, or someone, out my back window. I don't know if it was him, but it made me a little uneasy."

Someone was stalking Elise? His muscles tensing, Richard forced himself to relax and breathe. Elise needed him, or at least he hoped she would need him. No wonder she had all the security around her house. Richard took her hands in his. "Who is this guy? Did you call the police?"

"His name's Rolf Bitler. He was a fan who became overly obsessed. In California, I had to hire private security and take out a restraining order against him."

Richard squeezed her slender fingers. "How can I help? Do you need me to file another order here at the courts?"

"Thank you, but I took care of that at the police station earlier today. I also hired Valentino. He's looking into the situation. Hopefully, the eliminator will eliminate the Rolf problem." She gave a wry laugh.

"Man, Elise, I'm sorry you've had to deal with that." He pulled her into his arms. "Please let me know if there is anything I can do. Want me to camp out in your front room or sit outside the door to your bedroom and keep watch?" He'd fight that stalker and even fight dragons to keep Elise safe.

She rested her head on his shoulder. "I don't think that's

necessary, but that's sweet of you to offer."

Sending up a silent prayer for her protection, Richard held her close until her heart beat in time with his.

Chapter 20

"**I** wish you'd let me stay."

If it hadn't been Richard, Elise would have suspected ulterior motives. Trusting that he only wanted to keep her safe, she nestled in his arms as they stood in the foyer of her home. "I'm sure everything will be fine."

He kissed the top of her head. "If I go to my apartment, I won't get any sleep worrying about you."

"It was probably my imagination. For all I know, Rolf is still in California." Hopefully, that was true.

Richard held her tighter. "He better not be in Crawdad Beach. Call me if you need anything. I'm available day or night. I'm grateful you're using Valentino for protection."

"I'll let you know if anything happens, but I'm sure I'll be fine with him around. The local police know. Valentino notified several people in town who he said were also involved in personal security to keep watch." Which did make her wonder who that might be. "It's amazing that people who barely knew me are concerned for my safety."

"You have lots of people who care for you." Richard tilted her head up and gently kissed her lips. "You sure you don't want me to stay? I promise I don't have hidden motives. I just want you safe."

"Thank you, I'll be fine." Elise hoped her statement would reassure them both. "Valentino is outside watching right now. He's also monitoring my security system and has a key to the house if I need him."

Richard released her and took a step back. "With that big man on the premises, I guess I'd better behave."

"I need to talk to you about something else." They needed to discuss more than her physical safety.

He followed Elise to the living room and waited as she settled on the couch. He sat next to her, his gaze searching hers. "What do you want to talk about?"

"The possibility of a stalker again does make me a touch concerned about my physical safety."

"A *touch* concerned?"

Elise raised her chin. "I can take care of myself. I know martial arts and own a pistol."

"That's disturbing yet impressive information. Yet, you hired Valentino. What are you not telling me about this Rolf guy?"

Elise shrugged like it was no big deal. "He broke into my home in California one time."

Richard shot to his feet and moved next to her. "Were you there?"

"Thankfully, no. Rolf left notes taped around my house." Messages telling of his love. He left them on her refrigerator, television, bathroom, bed, and the worst one in her lingerie drawer.

Richard's eyebrows rose. "That's creepy, Elise."

"Yeah, I thought so too." She crossed her arms, wishing she could get rid of all those memories. "Enough about him. I need to take care of something else. I need to protect myself in other ways. During my singing career, as you know, I ran from my Christian upbringing and made a mess of my life. I can't do that again."

Elise took a deep breath before continuing. "After I returned to God, I've tried to live in a way that would please Him. Not because I think He will squash me like a bug if I misbehave again. God has had plenty of opportunities to do that."

She looked away from Richard's curious gaze. "I haven't dated in a long time because I didn't trust myself or men. I need to ensure that if I date again, I'm with someone who will draw me closer to God and not pull me away. I love the Lord and am so grateful to be His."

Having a conversation like this seemed surreal. A few years ago, she would have called herself a prude, but what she had now with God was deeper and richer. She loved and wanted to obey and please God.

Richard took her hands in his. "Elise, I'm not perfect. I've made tons of mistakes, but I'm back with God and want the same thing. I want to live a God-honoring life and be with someone who will make me a better man. And, I hope and pray you will take a chance on me."

A ridiculous, uncontrollable grin spread across Elise's face. "You want to be my boyfriend, lawyer-man?"

The dimple showed on Richard's cheek with his smile. "Only if you'll be my girlfriend."

"I would be honored to be the girlfriend of Richard Worthington, the third." Elise sealed that statement with a big kiss, and Richard seemed very happy to seal the deal with a big kiss of his own.

After promising Richard a zillion times she would take care of herself, he returned to his apartment. Elise set her security system to the home setting. That way, all windows and doors were in alarm mode, yet she could move around the house without problems. She'd made sure that when she had the system installed, Ian had the gate code to use as he needed.

Not ready to call it a night, she went upstairs to finish making that audiobook for her friend. The motion nightlights she'd installed around the house gave a soft glow as she carefully made her way upstairs.

It had been years since she had a boyfriend and way too long since she dated anyone decent. What would she have done if God wasn't a forgiving God?

She'd be dead or an absolute mess.

A rumble of thunder made her pause. No worries, she had soundproofed her recording studio.

Sitting in front of her microphone, Elise pulled her hair

into a ponytail.

Being raised by polite parents had been a blessing. However, she did not have healthy boundaries when she went off to pursue her singing career. She thought if she treated everyone courteously, everything would be fine. It was a harsh realization that not everyone was trustworthy. People used her to get ahead in the music industry, used her for their gains, and used her. Other people were just plain evil.

Hopefully, Richard and the friends she'd made in Crawdad Beach would be people she could trust.

Ready to start her recording, she switched her phone to the do-not-disturb mode.

Interesting. An unknown number had sent her a video.

She hit play.

No!

Rolf was out there.

Chapter 21

After forwarding the stalker video to Valentino, Elise locked her bedroom door, grabbed her gun, and watched the video again.

Rolf was standing at her front gate, talking about how he was looking forward to seeing her. Since the video hadn't been filmed at night, he must have been here while she was at the beach with Richard.

Why wouldn't Rolf leave her alone?

A text alerted her that Valentino was coming into the house. She remotely disarmed her security system.

"Elise!" Valentino's voice echoed from the foyer.

She peeked out of her bedroom door. "I'm in here."

His gaze alert, he hurried to where she stood. "I checked around your property and didn't see anyone. However, I noticed a car parked down the street. When I got close, the vehicle sped off. I was able to get the license plate number and notified the police." Valentino's eyes narrowed as he glanced at her pistol. "I assume you know how to use that?"

"I do." She kept the gun pointed at the floor and the safety on. "I grew up in the country and had plenty of target practice. I'm an excellent shot. I've also had martial arts training."

"Just make sure you know who you're aiming at before you squeeze the trigger," Valentino said.

"I promise." Elise hoped and prayed she'd never have to use her weapon.

"Have you thought about using a Taser instead of a pistol?"

"Oh, I have one of those and pepper spray."

His lips gave a fraction of a lift. "Stay locked in your room, and I'll check the house."

Elise sat on the edge of her bed. She thought she'd found a safe place. How had Rolf found her, and why was he harassing her again? She wasn't famous anymore.

But that probably didn't matter.

From what her California security team had told her, Rolf had a disturbing history. He'd never hurt anyone, but he had stalked other celebrities.

Maybe she should have returned to her hometown and lived close to her parents. But Rolf could have found her there and put her family in danger.

A knock brought Elise to her feet. She peered out at her protector.

"Your house is clear," Valentino said. "I didn't see any signs of tampering inside or out on your windows or doors. Would you like me to stay in the house tonight? You're not a sleepwalker, are you?"

"If you've checked everything, you don't need to stay

inside. I'll be fine. I won't leave my bedroom until morning."

"Set your security app to the home setting. Send me a text or call when you get up."

"Are you going to stay up all night?"

"You hired me to keep you safe, and I'll do whatever is necessary. I also have two friends stationed outside."

"Thank you. You know Ian may come back to his cottage, right?"

"We are aware of Ian. I contacted him earlier, and he won't be home for a few days." Valentino didn't explain how he had Ian's number. "Try to get some sleep."

Elise thanked him, locked her door again, crawled into bed, and turned off the lamp on her nightstand.

Knowing Valentino and his friends would keep watch gave her comfort, but how long would the threat from Rolf continue?

A bright flash of lightning illuminated the room, followed by a deep rumble of thunder. She rose to her feet and looked outside her window. A torrential downpour pounded against the glass.

When she was a kid, she used to love storms. Believing her parents would keep her safe, she'd burrow under her covers and fall asleep.

Now that she was older, she knew not all storms were caused by the weather.

Elise put on her robe and sat on the edge of her bed. She still believed God brought her to Crawdad Beach, and she wasn't about to give up her new home and her nice, handsome boyfriend without a fight.

Richard sat at his home office desk and stared at his computer screen. He'd prayed over and over again for Elise's protection, but he should have parked outside her house and kept watch instead of searching online for information on Elise.

Even though he hadn't closely followed her career, he was familiar with some of her music. The websites and the Wikipedia page listed under Elise's stage name stated that she'd retired due to throat surgery and remained a recluse in California.

The other information he discovered about her wild rock star years was more than he ever wanted to know. Richard shoved out of his chair. Rain pelting his windows, he stood by his French doors as flashes of lightning speared the earth.

What if people had followed him around, taking photos and posting about him all over the internet? He shuddered at that thought. He needed to remember Elise wasn't the same person as before.

Knowing what he now knew, even though she'd changed, how could he compare to the rich guys she'd dated? Would she miss the life she once had and want to return to her wild days? She'd traveled the world. What would she ever see in a small-town lawyer?

Richard stared out at the stormy night. Why was he worrying about Elise's past and how he might fit into her future? He should be more concerned about her safety.

A sudden screech of tires, followed by the rumble of a car's engine, drew his attention. A black-and-white police cruiser, its lights flashing and siren off, zoomed past and turned toward where Elise lived.

Richard ran to grab his car keys.

Chapter 22

Windshield wipers slapped against the onslaught of rain as Richard sped to Elise's house and screeched his car to a stop.

Strange. The police weren't here, but he'd seen them zoom past his apartment building. They'd even turned toward her street.

Did they leave their cruiser somewhere else so they could sneak up on that Rolf guy? What if the stalker was already inside Elise's house?

Richard switched off his car, pulled up his collar, and stepped into the rain.

Whomp!

Face down on the muddy ground, his arms pinned behind his back, Richard struggled to get air.

"What are you doing here?" A deep voice growled.

Was that Rolf? With a grunt of exertion, Richard lifted his head. "Who wants to know?"

Strong arms threw him on his back.

Dripping with rain, Valentino peered into his face. "Richard Worthington? What are you doing here?"

"Checking on Elise. I saw a police car with the lights flashing."

Valentino helped him to his feet. "They aren't here. It must have been something else. Elise didn't call you, did she?"

"No." Richard wiped the mud off his face. "I just wanted to make sure she's okay."

Valentino's gaze flicked to Elise's house. He blew a high and clear whistle that sounded like a cardinal's call. Two bird whistles answered. His gaze returned to Richard. "All's quiet here."

"You have two other people stationed around her house?"

"Yes. Now, please return home so we can keep our attention focused on Elise and her property."

"Right. Sorry about the interruption."

A slight smile crossed Valentino's face. "Don't worry, we'll take good care of her."

Water still dripping from his hair and clothes, Richard sat in his car and returned to his apartment.

As embarrassing as that was with Valentino, at least Richard knew Elise was in good hands. Even so, he would continue praying for her.

Paige's nose wrinkled. "That video is creepy; I felt a chill run down my spine while watching it."

"Yeah, I thought so too." Elise took her phone back.

Sir Purrcevel wrapped his tail around Elise's legs as

though providing comfort.

She rubbed his soft fur. "Thanks, Buddy. Thank you both for coming over."

Paige followed Elise into her living room. "Ursula told me today at work that Valentino was on duty last night at your house. I've been curious all day to find out what was going on. So, was everything okay?"

Elise waited until her friend settled on the couch, then sat beside her. Sir Purrcevel perched on the floor between them as though on guard duty.

"Everything is okay, but there was another incident. Valentino took down another man."

Paige's hand flew to her face. "Oh, my goodness. That's terrible."

Trying not to smile, Elise kept a straight face. "It was Richard."

"Richard was here to attack you?" Paige's voice rose an octave.

Sir Purrcevel let out a hair-raising growl.

"No," Elise chuckled as she stroked the big cat's soft fur. "Richard came to check on me, and Valentino didn't know it was him."

Paige chuckled. "That's too funny. It is sweet that Richard wanted to make sure you were okay."

"Yeah, it is. He's already called six times today and is coming over after work."

"We won't stay long. I'm dropping Sir Purrcy at Henry's

house for a play date with Filbert."

At the name of his dog friend, the big cat purred.

Elise motioned with her chin toward Sir Purrcevel. "Do you think he knows what is being said?"

Paige gave a slow nod. "He is very intelligent."

Elise leaned toward the cat. "If you ever see a guy named Rolf with a beard and long hair, would you make sure he doesn't bother me?"

Sir Purrcevel sat straight, his amber eyes fixed on her as though processing her statement. "Meow!"

"Thank you, kind sir. I feel safer."

"As well you should." Paige grinned as she stood and snapped the leash onto Sir Purrcevel's harness. "Take good care of yourself. Please let us know if there's anything we can do." She turned to go, but the big cat refused to budge. "Come on, we need to get going."

He moved close to Elise and stood by her side.

Paige tugged on the leash. "Filbert is waiting for us."

Sir Purrcevel's ears twitched, but he still refused to move.

Flabbergasted that he might be offering to stay to protect her, Elise leaned down to get close to his furry face. "You are very sweet, but I'm sure I'll be fine. Valentino and some of his friends will be here this evening to keep watch."

The big cat's gaze went from her, to Paige, to the front hallway, then back to Elise.

"Awww, I'll be okay. You don't have to stay with me."

He rubbed against her, then returned to his owner.

Paige stood there with eyebrows raised. “I know he’s smart, but I think he’s got a crush on you. I think we own the sweetest cat on the planet.”

Elise kissed Sir Purrcevel on his soft head. “Thank you for being a sweet kitty.”

Her phone signaled someone was coming through her unlocked front gate. Above a breathtaking bouquet of sunflowers, roses, and lilies, only the bright red peak of a baseball cap was visible.

Had Richard sent her another gift?

Paige peered over her shoulder at the camera app. “Wow, those flowers are gorgeous. Looks like things are getting serious with our town’s lawyer.”

“Yes, they are. We are officially dating.” Elise gave her friend a sassy look. “He should be coming over later.” She hurried to open the door for the delivery.

“These are for you.” The man handed her the flowers.

Rolf!

Chapter 23

A wave of icy fear washed over Elise. She stumbled backward, trying to distance herself from Rolf.

Wait a minute. She didn't have her gun, but she knew martial arts. Getting into a fighting stance, Elise focused, her breath slowing, preparing for action.

A hair-raising, menacing growl vibrated through the air behind her.

A flash of fur whooshed past Elise.

Sir Purrcevel launched himself onto Rolf's chest, knocking him backward and out the door.

Rolf screamed and writhed as the cat attacked with all four claws. "Help! Get him off me! Help!!!!!!"

"I called 911." Paige, her face serene, stood next to Elise. "Should I take my cat home?"

Elise took a deep breath, calming her racing heart. "Probably. Maybe wait a few minutes, though."

Valentino ran toward them and stopped beside Rolf. "Well, look what the cat dragged in."

"Help!" Rolf screamed. "I'm allergic to cats! Help!!!!"

Paige snapped her fingers. "Sir Purrcevel, that's enough."

The big cat halted his attack. His menacing growl rising in volume, he leaned close to Rolf's face.

The man squeezed his swollen, tear-filled eyes shut, a choked whimper escaping his lips.

With a firm tail thwack against Rolf's face, Sir Purrcevel sauntered toward Elise.

With a slight grin, Valentino hauled the groaning Rolf to his feet and shoved him forward. "I'll take care of what the cat left behind."

Still shaky from the adrenaline rush, Elise turned to Paige. "You can't imagine all the prayers I prayed about that situation."

"Are you okay?"

"I am now. It's all so surreal that it's over." Elise took a deep, cleansing breath. "All those years of worrying, hiring bodyguards, and wondering when Rolf would attack are finally over. Who would have thought all I needed was an assassin cat?"

Paige chuckled. "God works in mysterious ways."

"Yes, he does." Elise dropped to her knees and hugged her furry friend. "Thank you for saving me."

Sir Purrcevel responded with a loud, full-throttle purr.

Siren sounding and lights flashing, a police cruiser zipped past Richard as he walked to Elise's house.

Were they going to her house? With a surge of adrenaline, Richard took off running and turned down her street in time to see the officers exit their vehicle with guns drawn.

Frantically whispering a prayer for Elise's safety, Richard pushed past the other people, reaching her side and pulling her close. "Are you all right?"

She wrapped her arms around him. "I'm fine. Rolf will need medical attention, though."

Richard glanced at the man in Valentino's grip, surrounded by the two officers. Deep, bloody scratches covered Rolf's bearded face and arms, his eyes puffy and watering, his body jolting with violent sneezes.

"What happened to him?"

Elise grinned as she motioned with her chin. "My feline bodyguard, Sir Purrcevel, took matters into his paws."

Richard suppressed a chuckle. If he wasn't mistaken, the big cat standing next to Paige had a smirk on its furry face.

Chapter 24

"**T**his is the best day ever." It was over. Finally over. Elise let out a happy sigh as she munched on her soft roll. She was free of her stalker. Rolf was in police custody, facing multiple charges. She could live and enjoy her life.

Sitting across from her, Richard grinned as he paused his fork in midair. "I like Tiddlywinks, but I wish you'd have let me take you somewhere fancier to celebrate."

"Being in this wonderful little town with wonderful people, wonderful bodyguard cats, and eating in a wonderful restaurant with my wonderful new boyfriend is the best place to be."

"Howdy, Richard and Elise." Chester, holding a takeout container, stood next to their table. "I had to get a meal since Maybelline is at her book club tonight." He turned his mischievous expression toward Elise. "I heard you had some excitement."

"Yes, I did. However, my feline bodyguard, Sir Purrcevel, handled the situation for me."

"I heard the big cat left his mark, or should I say multiple marks." Chester chuckled.

Two teenage girls, talking loudly, entered the restaurant

and sat at a table behind them.

Elise stiffened when she heard the mention of her stage name.

"Coming here was a complete waste of time," one girl said, her voice dripping with boredom.

"But I saw a post last week that said she was here," commented the other girl.

A loud huff sounded. "If she *were* in South Carolina, why would she ever want to live in a tiny town like this after living in Los Angeles? She'd prefer someplace like Myrtle Beach, Hilton Head, or even Charleston."

Elise kept her head down and tried to focus on her food. Why couldn't she have one good day without worrying about her past coming back to haunt her?

Chester gave Elise's shoulder a gentle pat. "Excuse me for a moment." He stopped by the girl's table. "I understand you're looking for someone famous. We have Lucy Guthrie living in our town. She's known as Lawnmower Lucy because she won the Idaho Lawnmower Racing Championship."

"Okaaaay," said one girl.

"I told you," said the other. "She would *not* live here."

"You're probably right. Let's eat and drive to Myrtle Beach. There's a music festival there this weekend."

Chester leaned close to Elise's ear. "You'll be fine. We're protective of those who live in Crawdad Beach." He patted her shoulder, then walked away.

Richard squeezed her hand. "You okay?"

"Yes," Elise whispered. "Just frustrated." She had been feeling so good, and now? Listening to the girls was just a reminder that she would have to continue to be careful.

"Try to finish your meal." A playful grin stretched across his handsome face. "I've got an idea."

While they ate, the girls chatted about other recording artists they wanted to find.

Richard paid the bill, then stood and offered Elise his hand. "Come on, sugarplum." His voice went full Southern drawl. "We'd better get home to those six young'uns. Meemaw ain't gonna wanna watch them much longer. Not after Junior bit her last week."

Elise bit back a laugh as Richard led her to the door.

"I told you she would never live in a hick town like this," hissed one girl to the other as they passed their table.

Richard and Elise stepped outside and away from the restaurant window.

Pent-up laughter burst from Elise. "That was hilarious!"

Richard pulled her into his arms. "Give me a kiss, Sugar Plum."

She was happy to oblige with his request. "Thank you for providing me a not-so-graceful but very effective way to get out of the restaurant."

"I might not have the skills of Valentino or Sir Purrcevel, but I will do my best to keep you safe from rabid teenage fans. Come on, I'll walk you home."

Next to Richard, Elise grinned at him. "Your courage and

bravery are outstanding."

He wiggled his eyebrows. "You ain't seen nothing yet, Sugar Plum."

Elise's phone buzzed. She slid it out of her back pocket and checked the message. "Oh, my goodness! My friend who recorded my song said it will be released in the next few weeks."

"Your song?"

"Yes, I wrote a new song after I read Rosemary's journal. It's about how God takes our messed-up lives, forgives us, and gives us new opportunities." A wave of emotion at God's goodness washed over Elise, blurring her vision.

"I based it on Bible verses in Psalm 40 about God lifting us out of the mud, setting us on solid ground, and giving us a new song so that others would see the amazing things He has done."

Richard laced his fingers with hers, their hands fitting perfectly together as they walked side by side. "Sounds like a song many of us can identify with. Would you be willing to share it with me?"

Elise gave him a sly grin. "Only because, as a lawyer, you risked professional embarrassment by using a ridiculous drawl in the restaurant."

Richard's gaze shot to her face. "I hadn't thought about that. Great. Now the townspeople will think they have a hick for a lawyer."

They turned the corner of her street, and Elise nudged

him with her shoulder. "No, they won't think you're a hick. From now on, throughout Crawdad Beach history, they will tell of the handsome man who rescued a damsel in distress."

A slow grin spread across his face. "I've always wanted to be a hero in someone's story."

Elise blinked her eyelashes at him. "You and Sir Purrcevel are my heroes."

"Even though you ranked me with a cat, I'll take that as a compliment."

"Sir Purrcevel only received a hug and a pat. However, your heroic actions are unparalleled; thus, you deserve the unique expression of thanks conveyed through kisses."

Richard's deep chuckle reverberated in his chest. "Well, whenever you need a hero, just call."

"I can always use a hero."

He stopped, pulled her close, and gently kissed her.

She grinned up at him and, with her utmost heartfelt sincerity, expressed her gratitude to her heroic boyfriend.

Chapter 25

Elise stood in front of her full-length mirror. A flutter of excitement rushed through her, like happy butterflies dancing in her stomach. Tonight, she and Richard were celebrating four months together.

The soft cashmere of her dark blue V-neck cardigan dress felt luxurious against her skin as she secured her long hair in a stylish bun. Since the temperature had turned chilly, she added a classy blazer to complete the look.

This would be their first time visiting a restaurant outside Crawdad Beach. Hopefully, no one would recognize her.

Being with Richard was becoming increasingly difficult since they were trying not to cross a line in their relationship. During the warmer months, they would visit the beach or a nearby lake in the evenings when most people weren't around. Or they took long walks, hung out in her garden gazebo, or played games with other couples in town.

Now that winter had arrived, she and Richard spent more time indoors, and the temptation was getting crazy hard to ignore. She loved Richard, and knowing he loved her too still made her heart do that ridiculous sappy flutter like she was still a teenager.

Her phone app signaled Richard had arrived. Elise clicked to open the gate so his car could enter the driveway.

He stepped out of his vehicle wearing a stylish, fitted suit. It wasn't like she hadn't seen him dressed up before, but, oh my, he looked even more handsome this evening.

Heat rose to Elise's cheeks. Maybe she needed to hire Sir Purrcevel as a chaperone.

As Richard walked toward the door, she noticed a wrapped gift box about the size of a book in his hand. He was always bringing her something fun. She couldn't wait to see what he had brought her this time.

When she opened the door, he whistled. "Whoa, you look amazing."

Elise grinned. "You look mighty fine yourself, lawyer-man."

"Can I come in for a few minutes?"

"Of course." She closed the door behind him, then turned to him. "What's up?"

He took a deep breath. "I know we haven't been dating that long. And I'm not sure what an acceptable time limit is, but I love you, Elise, and I ..." he stammered. "I want to ask you something."

She raised her eyebrows. "Okay."

Richard thrust the box into her hands. "Open this."

She eyed him as she unwrapped what he brought. It was a brochure showing a cabin in the mountains. "You want to go to the Smokies?"

He grinned. "Yes. I found a secluded cabin where we could go without worrying about anyone seeing us."

"Just you and me?" Elise bit her lower lip. How could they keep their relationship from going places she didn't want to go?

"I want to be with you. Just you." Richard took her hands in his.

"But I thought we were trying not to spend too much alone time together."

"Elise, I don't want to wait anymore. I love you, and I want us to be together."

Her eyes misting with tears, she took her hands from his and turned away. "I love you, too. But not like this."

Richard didn't utter a sound, his silence deafening in the quiet room.

Tears gathering in her eyes, Elise stared at her living room fireplace. What was she going to do? She loved him, but what would happen if they became more physical in their relationship? Would he be like other guys? Love her and leave her? She didn't want to go through that kind of heartache again.

"Elise." She could feel his breath against her ear as he whispered. "I love you. Come away with me."

She shook her head. "I love you, too. But I want more than just a weekend away." Elise swiped the tears from her cheeks and wrapped her arms around herself.

She'd have to end the relationship, put new parameters

on him, or make a decision that would compromise who she wanted to be now. What was she going to do?

"Would you turn around, please?"

She took a shuddering breath. Might as well get it over with.

Elise turned. Her gaze dropped to where Richard was on one knee.

He held a small velvet box with a marquis-cut diamond ring toward her. "Elise Thomas, will you marry me? I want the cabin to be our honeymoon getaway."

Wide-eyed, she looked at the beautiful ring, then his handsome face. Richard had messed with her about the brochure. That stinker. "I can't marry you."

"What?" Richard's eyebrows raised. "Why not? I love you, and you said you love me."

"I do love you. But my full name is Elise Willow Thomas. If I marry you, I will become Elise Willow Worthington. My initials will be EWW."

Richard choked back a chuckle. "No, you will be Sugar Plum Elise Willow Worthington. Your initials would be SPEWW."

Elise laughed. "Yes, I'll marry you! How can I refuse having such excellent initials?"

He took the ring, placed it on her finger, and pulled her into his arms. "I can't wait to start our lives together."

"Me, too. I love you, Richard Worthington." She gave him a kiss filled with unspoken promises.

Richard moaned and gave her a kiss that made her knees weaken. "I vote for a very, very. brief engagement."

Elise grinned up at her handsome fiancé. "I strongly second that motion, counselor."

The End
of the story.
The beginning of their lives together.

"He lifted me out of the pit of despair, out of the mud and the mire. He set my feet on solid ground and steadied me as I walked along.
He has given me a new song to sing,
a hymn of praise to our God.
Many will see what he has done and be amazed.
They will put their trust in the Lord.
Oh, the joys of those who trust the Lord..."
(Psalm 40:2-4, NLT)

"The Lord your God in your midst,
the Mighty One will save;
He will rejoice over you with gladness,
He will quiet you with His love,
He will rejoice over you with singing."
(Zephaniah 3:17, NKJV)

Acknowledgments

Above all else, I give eternal gratitude to God, who lifts us from the slimy pit of our sinful mistakes and gives us a new life through his unending love, grace, forgiveness, and salvation. Thank You, God!

My sweet husband, Dennis, thank you for loving and marrying me. Thank you for your prayers, support, and encouragement. I'm so grateful God blessed me with you.

Patricia (Pacjac) Carroll, thank you for your insightful critiques, helpful feedback, and making the writing process even more enjoyable.

JoAnn Durgin, thank you for creating the beautiful cover. You are a blessing.

Jack Foster, thank you again for your creative Crawdad drawings used throughout the Crawdad Beach Series. (Readers, please visit Jack at jackfosterart.com)

Readers, thank you for taking the time to read *Elise's New Song.* I am very grateful to each of you.

If you liked the novel, would you be so kind as to leave a positive review and tell your friends? Thank you!

About the Author

Lisa Buffaloe is a happily married mom, speaker, and multi-published author.

Lisa enjoys spending time with God, Bible study, writing, hanging out with her sweet husband, and enjoying God's beautiful nature.

Please visit Lisa at https://lisabuffaloe.com, Facebook, X(Twitter), Instagram (buffaloelisa), Amazon, or GoodReads.

Books by Lisa

Fiction

Crawdad Beach Series

Visible, yet Hidden
Running to Grace
Crystal's Journey Home
A Baker's Heart
Stella's Heart Code
River Steps Free
Mia Lets Go
A New Paige
Running from Shame
Elise's New Song

Hope and Grace Series

Nadia's Hope
Prodigal Nights
Writing Her Heart
The Discovery Chapter
Open Lens

The Masterpiece Beneath
Grace for the Char-Baked

The Fortune

Non-Fiction

Float by Faith
Heart and Soul Medication
Time with The Timeless One
The Forgotten Resting Place
Present in His Presence
We Were Meant for Paradise
One Lit Step: Devotions for your journey
The Unnamed Devotional
Flying on His Wings
Unfailing Treasures
No Wound Too Deep For The Deep Love of Christ
Living Joyfully Free Devotional (Volumes 1 & 2)

Thank you for reading

Elise's New Song

Lisa Buffaloe

www.ingramcontent.com/pod-product-compliance
Lightning Source LLC
Chambersburg PA
CBHW061243170626
46809CB00007B/2800

* 9 7 8 1 9 5 7 7 1 5 4 4 5 *